To

your friend,

signature

oct/02

Wings of an Angel

WINGS OF AN ANGEL

Copyright © 2001 by Sigmund Brouwer

Published by coolreading.com, Red Deer, Alberta, Canada

Managing Editor: Mike Kooman.
Cover Art: Virginia Boolay – www.vboolayart.com

Canadian Cataloguing in Publication Data

Brouwer, Sigmund, 1959–
  Wings of an angel

ISBN 1-55305-032-0

  I. Title.
PS8553.R68467W56 2001   jC813'.54   C2001-910035-3
PZ7.B79984Wi 2001

Printed in Canada

Wings of an Angel

A Novel by
Sigmund Brouwer

Winds of Light Series
– Book 1 –

PROLOGUE

A.D. 1303

On a cold winter day in December, a feverish, starving man, barely clothed in rags, stumbled and fell at the door of a tiny and insignificant abbey in a small English county far north of London. A dusting of snow on the ground clearly showed drops of blood from the man's worn feet.

He did not live through the night, despite the hot broth offered helplessly by two old and befuddled monks.

The burden which the stranger left behind had nearly crushed the pitiful horse following him. It was a chest filled with books of strange writing. Both monks dutifully carried that chest to the abbey's library and stored it in a cobwebbed alcove.

Had either known of the significance of the books, that arrival would surely have been noted in the bulky diary of the abbey's monthly events.

However, poor and starving passersby were not unusual that long winter; the monks themselves faced enough difficulty trying to survive. The books were forgotten quickly in the harshness of living, and neither monk survived the winter. Each one was glad to surrender his soul to God after a weary and dull life on earth.

Other monks were eventually sent as replacements to tend the abbey with its sparse flock of sheep and rocky garden. They too had little interest in a neglected corner of the library.

Across the Channel, however, in the country of Franks later known as Germany, a man named Grey Friar Berthold Schwarz eventually took possession of a book missing from that collection.

He did realize how awesome and terrible its secrets might be.

As a result, in the year 1313, this German friar mixed charcoal, sulfur, and potassium nitrate and became known as the inventor of gunpowder – a substance which changed the history of western Europe, a substance which had already been used for centuries in China.

And at that English abbey, an orphan boy named Thomas had approached manhood.

Sigmund Brouwer

THOMAS
A QUEST REVEALED

SPRING A.D. 1312

Since dawn, each of the three ropes had hung black against the rising sun. Enough time had passed for a crowd to arrive and develop a restless holiday mood.

"Hear ye, hear ye, all gathered here today." The caller, short and dumpy with middle age, made no effort to hide the boredom in his voice.

His words had little effect on the restlessness of the hundred people crowded in front of the crude wooden gallows platform. Each person instead had eyes for the soon-to-be dead.

"Get on with your blathering, you old fool!" The shout came from a woman with a hungry face near the back of the crowd. A skinny child held her hand.

The caller man scratched at a flea beneath his dirty shirt and ignored her.

"This punishment has been ordered by the sheriff under authority of the Earl of York," he continued in a listless tone.

"The crimes to be punished are as follows." He unrolled a scroll and held it in front of him at arms length.

"Andrew, you dimwit! We all know you can't read. Don't be putting on airs for the like of us." This, from a fat man with jowls that shook as he yelled.

The crowd hooted with appreciation even though none of them, along with the speaker, realized the scroll was upside down. They grew quiet again.

And all stared at the soon-to-be dead.

Six burly soldiers stood behind the man with the scroll. In pairs, they held three prisoners tight. Too often, even the most weary prisoners made a sudden struggle for freedom when finally facing the thick rope which hung from the gallows.

It was a type of struggle the crowd hoped for. Hangings were now as common as weddings or funerals, so without a final bolt to escape or some howlings of despair, it would be a dull event. Indeed, this hanging only drew as many as it did because of the strange knight.

"John the potter's son. Found guilty of loitering with the intent to pick the pockets of honest men. To be hung by the neck until dead."

Most of the people in the crowd shook fists at the accused boy.

He grinned back at them. Ragged hair and a smudge of dirt covered the side of his face. "Intent!" he shouted in a tinny voice at the upraised fists. "Intent is all you could prove. I've always been too fast to be caught!"

Andrew waited for the noise to end and droned, "The unknown girl who does not speak or hear. Theft of three loaves of bread. To be hung by the neck until dead."

The crowd quieted completely as they stared at her. She in turn stared at her feet. High cheekbones and long dark hair hinted at a beauty to flower—if she were to live past the day.

That tragic air about her forced a mumble from the middle of the crowd. "The baker could have easily kept her for kitchen work instead of forcing the magistrate on her."

The baker flushed with anger. "And how many more mouths should I support in these times? Especially one belonging to a useless girl who cannot hear instructions?" he yelled back at his anonymous accuser.

Behind all of them—below the small rise of land, which held the gallows—the town known as Helmsley lay silent as the spring day began to warm. Although it was important enough to be guarded by a castle, the town was little more than a collection of wood and stone houses along narrow, dirty streets.

The stench of rotted wood in mud and of various barn animals filled the air. Few of the people gathered on the rise even noticed anymore.

Now, they fell as completely silent as the town. The strange knight was about to be formally accused.

"Finally"—Andrew in his dirty shirt felt the growing excitement of the crowd and his voice finally rose beyond boredom—"the knight who claims to be from a land of sun.

Found guilty of blasphemy and the theft of a chalice. To be hung by the neck until dead."

The babble of the crowd then renewed itself as each person strained to watch for reaction on the knight's haggard face. *To be so mighty and to fall so far...*

The darkly tanned knight did not acknowledge any curiosity. He had been stripped of all the wealth of his apparel except for his trousers, tunic, and a vest of chain mail. The bulges of his muscled arms and shoulders showed a man who had lived by the sword. And would die by the rope.

He did nothing except stare straight down with a bowed head that hid the features of his face.

Having stated all the charges, Andrew finished. "This on the 28th day of March in the year of our Lord thirteen hundred and twelve."

Finished with his painfully memorized words, he scrolled the useless paper back into a roll and nodded at the soldiers.

To the crowd's disappointment, none of the prisoners provided entertainment through resistance.

Each had a reason for not struggling.

The potter's son did not believe he might die. At seven years of age, death was simply not a possibility, even with the knotted rope less than a dozen steps away.

The girl was too exhausted.

The knight, resigned to death, was already back in his land of sun, speaking and laughing in his mind with old comrades.

Without any visible excitement available, the crowd grew restless. Some had neglected a day's work and traveled as far as six miles. Others had brought their entire families.

With all attention focused on the three figures slowly climbing the gallows, none in the crowd noticed a figure approaching from the town behind.

The figure strode amid the usual cursing and jeering and stopped the noise to an immediate awed silence.

As it should have been.

No man in the crowd stood higher than five feet and nine inches. This man was a giant, four hands taller than the tallest.

His attire cast a frightened chill among them. The black cloth, which swirled around him gleamed with richness and flowed like a heavy river. A hood covered his face; his hands were lost deep in the folds of the robe. He projected nothing less than the shadow of death.

The figure did not break stride until it reached the gallows. Only then did it stiffly turn to face the crowd, confident even with his back vulnerable to the soldiers.

Most in the crowd backed away.

Andrew, frozen in shock and standing on the gallows platform, still appeared shorter than the dark and terrible giant who had walked into their midst.

The huge specter of a man let the silence press down upon the crowd.

Finally, he uttered his first words.

"The knight shall be set free." His voice was unearthly, a deep rasping evil that sent the crowd back even farther. "He shall be set free immediately."

With those words, he extended his arms toward the crowd. Though unhurt, one of the children keened high with terror.

The black specter hissed.

Blue and orange flames shot outward from the right-hand sleeve of his robe.

Return the knight!" someone shouted. "Before we all die!"

"Andrew, save us!" pleaded another voice. "Set the knight free!"

Andrew blinked twice, then did something brave for a short, middle-aged man.

He pointed at the figure. "Seize the stranger!" he ordered the soldiers as his tongue unfroze.

Two stepped reluctantly forward and drew with both hands massive long swords.

The specter turned slowly and waited until the soldiers were nearly able to strike him.

"For your disobedience," the specter rasped clearly, "you shall become blind as trees."

He waved his left arm as if passing a blessing over the soldiers. Both fled the gallows, screaming and pressing their faces in agony.

"Do any others dare?" the specter faced and asked the crowd as the soldiers' screams faded.

Andrew, who may have been brave, but was not entirely stupid, issued fumbling orders to the remaining soldiers. They too withdrew weapons, but this time only short daggers to frantically saw at the ropes binding the knight.

The specter held his position entirely without motion.

Then, before the knight was entirely free, a bent and white-haired man draped in faded rags stepped forth. He limped steadily the last few steps until he faced the specter with an unfearing upward gaze.

"Your name is Thomas and you are nearly at complete manhood," he whispered so that only the giant specter could hear. Only his lips moved as he stared into the deep shadows of the black cowl. "And you shall give the crowd *my* instructions as if they came from your own mouth."

The specter did not reply. Did not move. To the rest of the crowd it was as if each figure were made of stone.

"Do you understand me, boy?" the old man whispered calmly. "Nod your head slowly, or I will lift that robe of yours and expose the stilts upon which you stand."

The nod finally arrived.

"Good." The old man's whisper remained the same. "Order the release of the other two prisoners."

Silence.

The old man smiled. "Surely, boy, you have no acid left to blind me. Otherwise you would have done so already. With nothing left to bluff the crowd, you must listen to me." His whispering intensified. *"Order their release!"*

The specter suddenly spoke above the head of the old man.

"Release the others or face certain doom," the specter's harsh voice boomed.

The old man chuckled under his breath. "As I thought. You are badly under equipped."

Andrew was unaware of the private drama between the specter and the old man, but grew brave at his continued safety. "All three?" he protested. "The sheriff will hang *me*."

"*Do as I say,*" the specter thundered.

Not a person moved.

"You are out of weapons, boy," the old man cackled quietly. "How do you expect to force them now?"

His question immediately became prophetic as, with no punishment coming from the specter, Andrew dared his question again. "All three? Impossible."

Murmurings came from the people as they too began to lose their edge of fear.

A rock, thrown from the back of the crowd, narrowly missed the giant specter.

He roared anger, but without flame or the cast of blindness, it was a hollow roar.

Another rock.

"Old man," Thomas hissed from black shadow. "This is your doing. Help me now."

The old man merely smiled and looked past the specter's shoulder at the sun.

"Raise your arms," he commanded.

One more rock whistled and struck the ground at their feet. Murmuring grew.

"*Raise them now,*" the old man repeated with urgency. "Before it is too late."

The specter raised his arms and the crowd fell silent as if struck.

He continued quietly to the boy. "Repeat all of my words. If you hesitate, we are both lost. There is less time remaining than for a feather to reach the ground."

The black hood nodded slightly.

"Do not disobey," he whispered. *"Tell them, 'Do not disobey.'"*

"Do not disobey." The heavy voice rasped with renewed evil.

"I have the power to turn the sun into darkness," the old man instructed.

"Impossible," the specter whispered back to him.

"Say it! Now!" The old man's eyes willed him into obedience.

So the specter's heavy voice boomed in measured slowness. *"I have the power to turn the sun into darkness."*

A laugh from the crowd.

The old man whispered more words, and the specter repeated each one slowly.

"Look over my shoulder," he said. *"I have raised my arms and even now you will see the darkness eating the edge of the sun."*

Another laugh, this time cut short.

Sudden gasps and assorted fainting spells in front of him startled the specter. He fought the impulse to look upward at the sun himself.

The old man gave him more instructions. The specter forced himself to repeat his words. *"Should I wish, the sun will remain dark in this town forever."*

He nearly stumbled at the words given him, because already the light of day grew dim. "What kind of sorcerer are you?" he demanded of the old man as he paused for breath.

The old man ignored him. *"All prisoners shall be released immediately,"* the old man replied, in a hypnotic whisper. "Tell them now while they are in terror."

Thomas did as instructed.

In the unnatural darkness, he heard Andrew and the soldiers scurrying into action.

Then he repeated the final words as given to him by the old man. "Send each prisoner from town with food and water. Tonight, at the stroke of midnight, the town mayor shall place a pouch of gold on these very gallows. The messenger I send for the gold will appear like a phantom to receive your offering. Only then will you be free of the threat of my return."

As the specter finished those words—trying hard to keep the wonder and fear from his own voice—unnatural darkness completely covered him and the gallows and the crowd and the countryside.

"You have done well, boy. Go now," the old man spoke. "Drop from your stilts and wrap your robe into a bundle and disappear. Tonight, if you have any brains in your head, you will be able to retrieve the gold. If not..."

In the darkness, the orphan boy named Thomas could only imagine the motion of the old man's hunched shrug.

"These prisoners?" Thomas whispered back. He wanted the knight more than he wanted the gold.

"You desired the knight. As you planned, he will be yours. *If* you prove to him you are his rescuer."

As I planned, Thomas wondered. *How did the old man know?*

In his confusion of questions, he blurted, "Why release the others?"

Around them, moaning of panic as the crowd fled in all directions.

The old man answered, "Take them with you. You will be guaranteed a safe journey to Magnus. And you must succeed, you *must* bring the winds of light into this age of darkness."

"You cannot possibly know of Magnus."

"Thomas, you have little time before the sun returns."

"Who are you!"

Thomas wondered later if there had been a laugh in the old man's reply.

These words came through the darkness, "The answer is in Magnus, boy. Now run, or you shall lose all."

or a man so big, approved Thomas as he slipped from tree to tree in pursuit, *the knight cuts through this forest like a roe deer.*

In contrast to the stiffness of the stilts Thomas had discarded less than an hour earlier, he now moved lightly on the leather soles strapped to his feet.

His tunic—crudely sewn and badly dyed coarse linen—fit him, almost it seemed, as tightly as his breeches. Normally that double reminder of poverty—clothes he must wear long after outgrowing them, and the brown of monk's charity cloth—irritated Thomas. On this occasion, while silently dodging branches, he was grateful for the brown which blended him against the background, and happy there was little loose material to snag on twigs and bark.

Thomas glanced up, seeking the sun's position by the light, which streamed dappled shadows onto the moss of the forest floor. He made a rough calculation.

Distance? *Already they were five miles east of Helmsley and the abandoned gallows.* Time? *Shortly before the sext bells which marked midday.* The half day of light remaining was ample to continue north and return to the abbey. *Yet were there enough hours left to secure the gold at midnight?*

Thomas decided he could not risk a delay in his plans. He reckoned the knight's forward progress, and began a wide circle through the falling slope of the forest to intercept him.

The deep moss soaked the sounds of his footfall, and he was careful to avoid the scattered dead and dry branches, which might crack loudly beneath his weight. Around him, vague sounds of birds echoed against the hush of the forest.

Some leaves were only buds. Others had been encouraged by the warm spring air to unfold. The splashes of green among trees long since tired of winter gave the forest an air of hope.

Thomas did not pause to enjoy the beauty. He concentrated on silent footstep after silent footstep, hoping he had remembered the lay of the land correctly.

Fifteen minutes later, Thomas grinned in relief at the expected wide stream at the bottom of the valley. While it blocked him, it would also block the knight. And a thick fallen tree appeared the one way to cross the water.

Thomas reached the primitive bridge and scrambled to its center above the water. He sat cross-legged and half hidden among the gnarled branches that bent and reached down into the stream, and waited.

The knight merely raised an eyebrow when he reached the bank of the stream and noticed Thomas among the branches of the log. His face, once hidden by a bowed head, now showed sharp shadows of the midday sun. Hair cropped short—no gray at the edges. Blue eyes as deep as they were careful to hide thoughts. Most compelling was the ragged scar down his right cheek.

He kept his eyebrow raised. "This appears to be a popular bridge for a forest so lonely."

Thomas smiled at the ironic tone of the knight's voice and added a touch of his own irony. "A shrewd observation, sir."

Thomas then stood and balanced in the middle of the fallen tree. He continued his smile. "I shall gladly make room for you to pass, sir. However, I beg of you to first answer a question."

Most men who had fought long and hard to reach the status of knighthood would have been enraged at such insolence. Most knights would have responded with a menacing steel blade. This knight simply permitted the slight curl of a grin to escape his face.

"You are an unlikely troll." The knight set down a large leather bag of food which he had been carrying over his shoulder, and contemplated Thomas. "That *is* legend in this country, is it not—the troll beneath a bridge with three questions to anyone who wishes to pass across?"

"I am not a legend," Thomas answered, then added boldly, "but together, we may be."

They stared at each other in a silence pleasantly broken by the burbling of the stream between them.

The knight saw a slim but square shouldered boy, dressed in the clothing of a monk's assistant, who did not flinch to be examined so frankly. Ragged brown hair tied back. High forehead to suggest strong intelligence. A straight noble nose. And a chin that did not waver with fear at a strange knight's imposing gaze.

The knight almost smiled again as he noted the boy's hands. Large and ungainly, they protruded from coarse sleeves much too short. *A puppy with much growing to do*, the knight first thought with amusement, *at that awkward age between boy and man.*

What checked the knight from smiling was the steady grace promised in a relaxed stance. And the depth of character hinted by gray eyes flecked with blue that stared back with calm strength. *Does a puppy have this much confidence*, the knight wondered, *this much steel at such a young age?*

Then the knight did grin. *This puppy was studying him in return with an equal amount of detached curiosity.*

"I presume," the knight said with a mock bow, "I pass your inspection."

Thomas did not flush as the knight expected. He merely nodded gravely.

Strange. Almost royal. As if we are equals, the knight thought. He let curiosity overcome a trace of anger and spoke again. "Pray tell, your question."

Thomas paused, weighing his words carefully. On his next sentence, he knew, the future of his life depended.

"Does your code of knighthood," Thomas finally asked, "make provisions for the repayment of a life saved and spared?"

The knight thought back to his tired resignation in front of the gallows, then to the powerful joy, which followed to be spared by the miracle of the sun blotted by darkness.

"If there is nothing in this code you speak of," the knight said slowly as he pictured the heavy ropes of his death hanging against the dawn sky, "I assure you there certainly should be."

Thomas nodded again from the center of the log. He fought to keep tension from his voice. *Never would he have this opportunity again. And the childhood songs from a tender nurse haunted his every dream...*

"Sir William," Thomas cast his words across the water, "consider me with kindness, I beseech, in the regretful necessity which forces me to ask repayment of that debt from you."

On a normal day, the knight would have merely chuckled at such an absurd claim.

It was not a normal day.

Only hours earlier, Sir William had prepared himself to die with dignity, and such effort is not easy. The mix of emotions he had been holding inside after the sudden escape from death needed release.

That mix of emotions found release in white-hot rage.

So his swift reaction—not the bemused questions as Thomas had expected—was stunning.

"Insolent whelp!" roared the knight.

In one savage movement, he surged onto the log and lunged at Thomas. His bare hands flashed. Fingers of iron tore into Thomas' paralyzed flesh.

"I'll grind you into the worm's dust," the knight vowed as he tightened fingers around the neck in his gasp. *"To follow me and lay such a pretentious claim..."*

Inhuman rage prevented Sir William from continuing his words. Instead, his biceps bulged with quick hatred as he began to lift Thomas by the throat with both of his war-hardened hands.

Unable to speak, Thomas did the only thing he could do. Eyes locked into eyes, he waited for the knight's sanity to return.

The knight only roared an animal yell of no words and lifted higher.

Blackness began a slight veil across Thomas' vision.

He brought a knee up in desperation. It only bounced off chain mail stretched across the knight's belly.

Still, Sir William squeezed relentlessly.

The blackness became a sheet. *I... must... explain,* Thomas willed to himself. *One... last... chance.* He reached for one of the gnarled branches of the fallen log. *If... this... breaks... I... am... dead...*

He did not waste energy to complete the thought. With his final strength, Thomas pulled hard on the branch. It was not much. The knight's rage had already drained too much life from his bursting lungs. But it was enough.

Sir William—already in an awkward position with Thomas held extended in midair—did not anticipate the tug on his balance. Both toppled sideways into the stream from the log.

Thomas nearly made the fatal mistake of gasping for air as the iron hold on his throat vanished. Instead, he bucked against the water and fought for the surface. His feet slammed bottom in the waist deep water, and he sucked in a lungful of air.

He looked for the knight, prepared to scramble for land.

Instead of a charging bull, however, he saw only the matted cloth of the knight's half submerged back.

Thomas reacted almost as swiftly in concern as Sir William had moments earlier in anger.

He thrashed through the water and pulled the man upward. Immediately, the reason for the man's state became obvious. An ugly gash of red covered the knight's temple.

Thomas winced as he noted a smear of blood on a nearby boulder.

He dragged the man to shore, ripped a strip of cloth from his shirt, and began dabbing at the blood.

Within seconds, Sir William groaned.

He blinked himself into awareness and looked upward at the boy.

"By the denizens of Hades," Sir William said weakly, his sudden rage vanished. "This cannot mean you now have *really* spared my life."

❦

They began to speak as their shirts dried among the branches.

"You left the pickpocket and the girl at the road." Thomas made it a statement. "And you seek to hide in the forest."

"You followed me," Sir William countered as he hopped and slapped himself with both arms against his cold wet skin. "And don't think because I am not strangling you again that I accept your story about the rescue at the gallows."

Thomas moved back to place several more cautious yards between them.

"I was that specter," he said.

Sir William laughed. "Look at you. A skinny puppy drenched to the bone. Not even as high as my shoulders. And you claim to be the specter who brought darkness upon the land."

The knight shivered, but not from the chill of the spring air. He then crossed himself reverently. "Such a miracle I have never heard proclaimed."

Thomas could say little to that. He himself could still only half believe the events of the morning.

"I was that specter," he persisted. "I stood upon stilts, covered by a black robe and..."

The knight moved to a patch of sunlight. His white legs gleamed. "Don't bother me with such nonsense," he growled. "I heard the specter speak. Your voice is a girl's compared to the one that chilled the crowd."

Thomas hugged himself for warmth. It seemed that now a complete silence swallowed them as they shivered in the depths of the forest.

"I spoke through a contraption designed to conceal my voice," Thomas began to explain.

Again the knight waved him into silence. "I see that none of these inventions are with you."

"I needed to find you quickly," Thomas protested. "I barely had time to hide my bundle."

"How old are you, boy?"

"Fourteen."

"Fourteen," the knight repeated darkly. His voice rose. "Fourteen!"

Sir William paused to let his anger grow. "You try my patience, puppy. No man—let alone a half-grown man—has the power to shoot flame from his hands or cast blindness upon the sheriff's best men."

Sir William drew himself up. "And no man," he said with renewed anger, "has the power to bury the sun." He touched his forehead and brought his finger down to examine the blood, then scowled. "If you continue to insist upon these lies, I shall soon forget you pulled me from the stream."

Thomas paused halfway through the breath he had drawn to reply. The forest was silent. Hadn't the muted cries of birds been a backdrop for most of their time among the trees?

Thomas held up a hand and cocked his ear for sound.

"Did the hangman make any suggestion that you would be followed?"

Sir William shook his head in irritation, then scowled again at the renewed burst of pain. "None. The man was as cowed as any of the villagers. He fairly cried with relief to see me on my way."

They stared around them. Thomas hugged himself harder to fight the chill of wet skin against spring air.

"I swear to you, Sir William," he said in a low voice. "I was that specter. And I beg you give me the chance to prove it."

"For what reason. I don't even know who you are."

"My name is Thomas. I have been raised north of here, on the fringe of the moors, at a small abbey along the Harland Moor."

The knight snorted. "A stripling monk"

Thomas shook his head. "Never a man of

the church. And with your help, something much more. The help, I humbly add, that you have already promised to the person who saved you from the gallows."

Sir William waved a fist in Thomas' direction. He dropped it in frustration.

"Thomas of Harland Moor," he announced heavily. "Here is my word. Show me the pouch of gold to be taken at midnight from the gallows—which I assure you will be heavily guarded—and deliver it to me tomorrow in the guise of the specter. Then I shall be in your debt. Failing that—as you surely shall—give me peace."

Thomas grinned elation in response. In his careful planning of this day, he had never expected to be shivering and bare-chested and waiting for his clothes to dry as he heard the words he wanted so badly. Still, his quest was about to begin, and only a fool looked a gift horse in the mouth to check for worn teeth.

His thoughts turned, as they always did, to the childhood songs repeated evening after evening by the one person at the abbey who had shown him compassion and love.

So much to be fulfilled...

A giggle interrupted his thoughts.

Sir William reacted again with that unexpected swiftness for a man so large and sprang in the direction of a quivering bush.

There was a flurry of motion and a short struggle.

Then Sir William straightened. He held them by the nape of the backs of their shirts, the pickpocket and the mute girl.

Thomas reached for his damp shirt to cover his naked chest from the girl's dark eyes. Then he wondered suddenly why he wanted to stare back in return. He had seen many of the village girls before, always ignoring their coy glances as he accompanied the monks to market. Fourteen was an age when already some began to consider marriage. Thomas had a future to find, the one given to him during his childhood songs and fables. No girl had tempted him to look beyond that future. *This one...*

He shook his head at the distraction and fumbled to pull the shirt across his chest. There was barely time to return to the abbey and he had much more to accomplish by midnight.

Sir William walked forward with his double burden. Disgust was written plainly across his face.

The dirt-smudged pickpocket shook uselessly to free himself. "People, they shouted curses at us along the road. Threw stones and called us devil's children," he said mournfully from his perch in the air. "What had we to do but come follow?"

Sir William sighed long and deep and set them down with little gentleness.

Chapter Five – Part One

As Thomas reached the summit of the final moor before the abbey, bells rang for *none*, the time of church service three hours past midday. If one could fly with the straightness of a crow, the Harland Moor Abbey was barely six miles due north of his meeting place with the knight. Winding footpaths and caution against roaming bandits, however, had made his travel since then seem more like twelve miles. Despite that, he had moved with a quickness driven by urgency.

Now, ahead and below in the valley, Thomas could see the cold stone walls of the abbey hall, blurred as they were by the trees towering in front. The valley itself was narrow and compressed, more rock and stunted trees on the slopes than sweet grass and sheep—probably the only reason it had been donated to the mother abbey by an earl determined long ago to buy his place in heaven. The mother abbey at Rievaulx, just outside of Helmsley, was part of the large order of Cistercian monks, and had always accepted such gifts. With this one, Rievaulx had quickly established an outpost designed to earn more money for the church. Time had proven the land too poor, however, and barely worth the investment of abbey hall, library, and living quarters made from stone quarried directly from the nearby hills.

Thomas moved quickly from the exposed summit into the trees lower down near the tiny river, which wound past the abbey. Years of avoiding the harsh monks had taught him every secret deer path in the surrounding hills. At times, he would approach a seemingly solid stand of brush, then slip sideways into an invisible opening among the jagged branches and later reappear quietly farther down the hill.

His familiarity with the terrain, however, did not make him less cautious. Especially since his first destination was not the abbey itself, but a precious hiding place away from the monks.

Several bends upstream from the abbey hall, comfortably shaded by large oaks, there stood beside the water a jumble of rocks and boulders, some as large as a peasant's hut. Among them, a freak of nature had created a dry cool cave, its narrow entrance concealed by jutting slabs of granite and bushes rising from softer ground below.

Thomas circled it once. Then he slipped into a nearby crevice and surveyed the area.

Count to one thousand, echoed the instructions which had been given him time and again. *Watch carefully for movement, and count to one thousand. Let no person ever discover this place.*

Thomas settled into the comforting hum of forest noises, alert for any sign of intruders, and pondered the day,

First, he would need the power of knowledge hidden within the cave. Then, time to assemble that power. Thomas half smiled. *So much waiting inside among the books...*

Enough time had passed. He circled slowly once more, remembering, the way he did every time, the love someone had given him with the instructions he had repeated back endlessly.

Never, never speak of the existence of the books. Always, always, be sure beyond doubt no person sees you slip into the cave. The books have the power of knowledge beyond price. Take from them, and never, never speak of their existence.

As Thomas entered the coolness of the artificial cave, sadness overwhelmed him with the darkness. Because it never failed to remind him of the one who had so patiently taught.

He stood motionless, steadying his breathing until his eyes adjusted to the gloom. He waited another fifteen minutes. Then he moved forward to the shaft of sunlight that fell between a large, crack of one slab leaning crookedly against another.

With little hesitation, he pulled aside a rotting piece of tree that looked as if it had grown into the rock behind it.

Thomas dragged out a chest that was as high as his knees and as wide as a cart. He opened the lid, reached inside, and gently lifted out a leatherbound book the size of a small tabletop.

He searched page after page, carefully turning and setting down each leaf of ancient paper before scanning the words before him.

Nearly an hour later, he grunted with satisfaction. There *was* a way to get the gold.

Without hurry, he returned the book into the chest, then the chest into its spot in the stone, then the lumber in front of the chest.

Thomas silently counted to one thousand at the entrance of the ruins before edging back into the forest.

No supper for you tonight," wheezed Prior Jack with vicious satisfaction as he pinched Thomas's right ear between stubby thumb and forefinger.

Thomas did not move. The only sound in the abbey hall, then, was a slight scuffling of Prior Jack's feet as he balanced his huge bulk on the stone floor.

Prior Jack was disappointed not to find immediate fear in the boy.

"I've changed my mind." Prior Jack's eyes became pinpoint dots of black hatred almost hidden in rolls of flesh. "You're finally to the age which lets us consider flogging instead, you ignorant peasant orphan."

Thomas closed his eyes and fought pain and anger. *Today is my last day here. It shall be fortunate if I don't murder this man...*

Prior Jack's permanent wheeze—while speaking or even breathing—resulted from the gross fatness which also forced him to waddle sideways through most of the abbey's narrower doorways.

Once, on a sweltering summer day, Thomas had heard splashing in the pond behind the abbey. He'd crept closer, and seen Prior Jack waist deep in the water. So wide and blubbery were the rolls of stark white fat that Thomas could barely recognize the shape of a man beneath the boulder head.

Not that fatness was unfashionable. On the contrary, it was a status symbol. Only the rich could afford it. Most of the peasants suffered from continuous hunger, and considered themselves fortunate each day to eat more than a bowl of thin cabbage soup and some slices of black wholemeal bread, never with butter.

It had angered Prior Jack immensely to see Thomas slipping through the back hall of the abbey, because it meant that, once again, Thomas had neglected his work in the garden. The soil was poor enough already to irritate a man of his girth. Without the boy's constant work—unless Prior Jack cut down to five meals a day—fall's harvest would only last until January.

Worse, no one knew to where the boy disappeared. Often Prior Jack or one of the other three monks had tried following, but it was as useless as tracking smoke from a fire. All they could do—and all they ever did—was punish him on his return.

Not once did they guess how badly the method had backfired. In efforts to escape over the years, Thomas had learned secret ways through the old abbey and hidden paths on the abbey grounds. Worse for the monks, he had been forced to learn how to move quietly. The continuous punishment had made Thomas the perfect spy and had toughened him to endure anything.

Quiet or not, within the abbey itself, Thomas did not always escape Prior Jack's quick mean hands and silent padding feet. This was not the first time the monk had managed to sneak close enough to grab his ear.

But it would be the last, Thomas vowed to himself.

"Prior Jack," Thomas said from gritted teeth as he reached into his shirt. "You are a fat, obscene pig." Thomas pulled his hand free. "If you don't let go, this knife will slice lard off you in strips."

Prior Jack rattled a gasp from his overworked lungs. "How dare you threaten me. I am a man of God!"

Regardless of that claim of status, Thomas noted, the monk had dropped his grip and stepped back quickly enough. Thomas took a deep breath of his own. He finally spoke the words he had been dreaming and rehearsing.

"You? A man of God? First convince me that God exists. Then convince me you're a man, not a spineless pig of jelly. And finally, if God does exist, prove to me that you actually follow Him instead of preaching one thing and doing another."

The fat monk's cheeks bulged in horror. For years, the boy had only responded with defiant silence. It curdled his blood to suddenly hear this, and then see, like steel revealed behind a falling cloth, that the scrawny boy and his corded muscles had grown close to manhood without it being noticed.

Resolve had changed the boy's eyes, the monk decided in fear. The gray in them had become ice and the knife in his right hand did not waver.

"Matthew! Frederick! Walter!" Prior Jack bellowed into the empty stone corridors. He took a step farther back from Thomas and dropped his voice to its usual strained wheeze. "Put the knife away. Immediate penitence may spare your soul after such blasphemy."

Dust danced between them, red and blue in the glow of the light beams from a stained glass window on the west side of the corridor. It reminded Thomas that the sun indeed was at a sharp angle. Eventide would be upon him soon.

His plan must work. And there was little time to complete it. Yet, first he must get past this detestable bully, and the three other monks he could hear scurrying toward them. Would he actually murder to obtain his freedom?

They arrived almost immediately, shaved heads faintly pink from exertion.

"The boy has lost his mind," Prior Jack whined. "As you can plainly see, he is threatening to kill me."

Monk Walter, gaunt and gray, frowned. "Put the knife down, boy. Now. And you will only be whipped as punishment. If not, you will lose your hand."

Thomas knew that was no idle threat. Peasants *had* had their hands cut off for a simple crime like theft. To threaten members of the clergy was unimaginable.

"Tonight," Thomas said calmly instead of dropping the knife, "is the night you set me free from this hole that is hell on earth. Furthermore, you will send me on my way with provisions for a week, and also three years' wages."

"Impertinent dog," squeaked Monk Philip. Tiny and shrunken, he quickly looked to the others for approval. "You owe us the best years of your life. Few abbeys in this country would have taken in scum like you and raised you as we did."

"As a slave?" Thomas countered. He lifted his knife higher, and they kept distance. "Since I was old enough to lift a hoe, you sent me to the garden. When I cried because of raw blisters, you cuffed me on the head and withheld my food. Your filth—dirty, stinking clothing and the slop of your meals—I've cleaned every day for seven years. Winters, I chopped wood mornings while you slept indoors, too cheap to give me even a shawl for my blue shoulders."

Monk Frederick rose on his toes and pointed at Thomas. His greasy face turned red with indignation. "We could have thrown you to the wolves!"

Thomas spat at their feet.

"Listen to me, you old feeble men." In saying that, Thomas felt a surge of hot joy. The moment was right, he knew without doubt. The hesitation that had filled him with agony for six months had disappeared.

Yes, he had been ready to leave for some time. The words of his childhood nurse had echoed softly during the dark hours as he lay in bed, night after night, dreaming of this moment. But he had waited and endured until, as the nurse had promised, the day arrived when he could make best use of all the weapons of intelligence and strength that she had given him before her death.

Then a day had arrived with news of a scheduled hanging of the knight, and a vision of his future had filled him. During the busy hours of daylight over the last week, again, the words of his childhood songs had echoed as he had prepared carefully to ensure the moment would indeed belong to him.

And it did.

isten," Thomas repeated. "You did not take me here as charity. You took me because the Prior at Rievaulx ordered that you take me and the nurse. He did so because my parents were not peasants as you have tried to lead me to believe. My father was a mason, a builder of churches, and left behind enough money to pay for my education among the clergy. Yet you took advantage of the distance from the abbey at Rievaulx and instead of providing education, used me as a slave."

Monk Philip glanced wildly at the other three. "He cannot know that," he sputtered.

"No?" Thomas' voice grew ominous. As he spoke, he began to see by the reactions of the monks how much strength he had carefully hidden from them, and, to his surprise, from himself.

"No?" Thomas spoke quietly enough to make them strain for every savage word. "The letters you leave carelessly about speak plainly to me. I've read every report—every false report—that you have sent to the Prior at Rievaulx. Would it were that I was half as content as you have made him believe."

Monk Walter shook his head. "You cannot read. That is a magic, a gift the clergy give to very few."

Thomas ignored him. "Furthermore, I have written in clear Latin a long letter which details the history of this abbey over the last years. To be certain, I have also transcribed the letter into French, with that copy reserved for the Earl of York."

"He writes too?" gasped Monk Philip. "Latin *and* French?"

"These letters are in the hands of a friend in the village. Unless I appear tonight to ask them back, he will deliver them to the mother abbey. All of you will be defrocked and sent penniless among the same peasants you have robbed for years without mercy."

"It's a bluff," Prior Jack declared. "If we all move at once, we can lay hold of him and deliver him to the sheriff—for hanging."

Time ebbed heartbeat by heartbeat in the stillness of the abbey.

Thomas held up his hand and the sudden motion checked any rash action. "Monk Frederick. Your accounting of the wool taken from the sheep that I guarded night after night. Will it bear close scrutiny when the Prior at Rievaulx sends men to examine the records? Or will they discover you have been keeping one bag of wool for every ten sold, and turning the profit into gold for yourself?"

Frederick's face grew white.

"Don't worry," Thomas said. "The strongbox you have hidden in the hollow of a tree behind the pond is safe. But empty of your gold. That has already been distributed among the villagers to hold my letter."

The other monks swiveled their heads to stare at Frederick

"I see," Thomas said. "A secret from the others."

A growl from Prior Jack proved it true.

"Prior Jack," Thomas snorted. "The menial tending of dishes you forced upon me after each meal made my observations very easy. That letter also details the food you consume in a single month. I'm sure the Prior at Rievaulx will be disappointed to discover that you slobber down nearly 400 eggs from full moon to full moon. Over fifty pounds of flour. Three lambs. And a side of beef. It will explain, of course, why this abbey has not made a harvest contribution to the mother abbey in five years."

Prior Jack's cheeks wobbled with rage.

"Tut, tut," Thomas cautioned. "Anger, like work, may strain you badly."

"Enough," Monk Walter said.

"Enough? Is it because you dread to hear what that letter reports of you?"

The lines of Monk Walter's face drew tight. "You shall get your provisions."

"This means, I take it, that your fellow monks don't know *your* secret vice?"

"You will also receive three years' wages," Monk Walter said.

"He's a male witch," Thomas said simply to the other three. "A practicing warlock.

Potions, magic chanting, and the sacrifice of animals at midnight."

The three monks recoiled from Monk Walter.

"Oh, don't worry," Thomas said. "He's quite harmless. I've heard the man sobbing into his pillow from failure more times than I care to recall."

In the renewed silence, they could only stare at each other. Four monks in shabby brown. A full grown boy with enough calm hatred to give him strength.

"I will take my wages in silver or gold." Thomas was the first to break the impasse. "Have it here before the sun is down, along with the provisions. Or I shall demand *four* years' wages instead."

They hesitated.

"Go on," Thomas said. "I'll keep my word and have the letter returned to you tomorrow—when I reach the village safely."

They turned and scurried, but even before rounding the corner of the hall, had already begun heated arguing and accusations.

The last rays of sun warmed the stained glass as Monk Walter and Monk Philip strode back to Thomas.

Monk Walter held out an oily leather bag. "Cheese, bread, and meat," he said. "Enough to last you ten days."

Monk Philip tossed Thomas a much smaller sack. "Count it," he said. "Two years in silver. Another year in gold."

Thomas regarded them steadily. Where was the fear with which they had departed barely a half hour earlier? Why the gleam of triumph behind Monk Walter's eyes?

"Thank you," was all Thomas said as the comforting weight of both sacks dragged on his arms. Yet he waited before leaving. An unease he could not explain filled him.

"Go on, boy," Monk Walter sneered in the gathering darkness of the hall.

Still Thomas waited. Unsure.

Monk Philip gazed at the rough stones beneath his feet.

"In the letter," Monk Philip mumbled. "What have you to tell the Prior at Rievaulx about me?"

Thomas suddenly felt pity. The tiny man's shoulders were bowed with weariness and guilt.

"Nothing to damn you," he said gently.

"Nothing to praise you. As if you merely stood aside all these years."

"You show uncanny wisdom for a boy," Monk Philip choked with his head still low. When he straightened, he made no effort to hide tears. "Perhaps that is the worst of all, not to make a choice between good or evil. I'm old now. I can barely hear, yet the slightest noise wakens me from troubled sleep. My bones are brittle and I'm afraid of falling, even off the chapel steps. The terrifying blackness of death is too soon ahead of me."

"Quit your blathering," Monk Walter said between clenched teeth. "Send the boy on his way. Now!"

Monk Philip clamped his jaw as if coming to a decision. "Not to his death. Nor shall I meet God without attempting some good." He drew a lungful of air. "Thomas. Leave alone the—"

Monk Walter crashed a fist into the tiny man's mouth. The blow drove Monk Philip's head into a square stone, which jutted from the wall. He collapsed to his knees without a moan.

Monk Philip smiled once at Thomas,

struggled to speak, then toppled from his knees and did not move.

Thomas felt a chill. *What had Philip been trying to say?*

"Spawn of the devil," Monk Walter hissed at Thomas. "Your soul will roast in hell."

Thomas said nothing, and rested the bag of food on his shoulder. He took a half step away, then turned to deliver a promise.

"Monk Walter," he began with quiet deadliness, guessing suddenly the reason for Philip's death. "If indeed there is a place as hell, your soul will be there much sooner than mine. And the guilt shall be upon your shoulders as surely as the death of your brother here."

Thomas then left the hall as silently as his shadow. He paused outside until the noises inside told him that the three remaining monks were struggling with Monk Philip's body. Then, to fulfill his parting promise, Thomas slipped to the rear of the abbey into the cool storage room dug below the kitchen.

Had the monk meant leave alone—the food? Thomas departed shortly after into the darkness, climbing the valley hills with one fewer sack than he had planned. *If indeed they had poisoned his provisions in an attempt at murder, they would eat judgment upon themselves.*

ompline. Already.

Every three hours the small village church rang its bells to let the people mark the passage of time. Each new ringing from the small village church marked a different devotion for the clergy. *Matins* at midnight, *lauds* next at three a.m., and so on. The eighth ringing of the bells meant the last service of the day, *compline*—nine p.m.

That clanging of bronze clappers against bronze bells reached Thomas clearly where he sat, arms hugging knees, beneath a tree halfway between the village and the gallows.

Compline. Already.

Three bundles now lay beside him. One, a small sack with gold and silver given by the monks. The second, from his efforts in the cave that afternoon. And the third, the bundle of stilts and cloth he had recently recovered from its earlier burial place near the gallows.

Thomas could do no more to prepare himself for his next test. Yet the waiting skimmed too quickly.

He merely had to turn his head to see the distant gallows occasionally etched black against the light of moon when it broke through uneven clouds.

If I could pray, Thomas thought, *I would pray for the clouds to grow thicker. Clear moonlight will only make my deception more difficult.*

The gold was not in place yet. That he knew. He had chosen this place to hide because it was near the road that wound out of Helmsley. It would let him see how many men the sheriff sent from the village as they guarded the gold on its short journey.

Not for the first time in the last few cold hours did Thomas wonder about the mysterious old man. In front of the panicked crowd in the morning, he had taken great pains to force Thomas to demand gold that was more money than five men could earn in five years. Enough to provision a small army.

Almost as if the old man had read Thomas' mind.

Thomas shivered. Not because of cold.

How had he known Thomas was not a specter, but an imposter on stilts? How had the old man known what Thomas wanted? And how had the old man deceived them all with a trick of such proportion that it had appeared the sun had run from the sky?

With those final questions to haunt him, Thomas discovered that time could move slowly. Very slowly indeed.

"I'll not rest until this gold has been safely borne away by the specter."

The voice reached Thomas dearly in the cold night air. By reflex, he put his hand on the bundles. Reassured by their touch, he listened hard.

"Fool!" a harsh voice replied. "The sheriff has promised a third of this gold to the man who brings down the specter. I, for one, have sharpened my long sword."

"I'm no fool," the first voice replied with a definite tremble. "I was there when the sky turned black. The ghostly specter is welcome to his ransom. I only pray we never see him again."

"Shut your jaws!" commanded a third voice. "This is a military operation. Not a gathering of old wives."

With that, only the drumming of heavy feet.

Thomas counted eight men in the flitting moonlight. Eight men!

As much as he might take joy in the way his muscles seemed to respond more and more to hard work during the day, he swallowed fear to remind himself that he had yet to shave a full growth of beard.

Was he a village idiot to think he might overcome the odds of eight well-trained sheriff's men? And if he did succeed at midnight, what might he face next in the months to come?

Again, Thomas regretted briefly that he could not pray.

Instead, he silently sang lines from a chant that had so often comforted him in his childhood.

Delivered on the wings of an angel,
he shall free us from oppression.
Delivered on the wings of an angel,
he shall free us from oppression.

The last of the footsteps faded.

As the clouds came and went, Thomas snatched glimpses of men setting themselves in a rough circle around the gallows.

The bells for *matins* began to ring from the village.

Exactly midnight.

The promised phantom did not keep the sheriff's men in suspense.

It appeared as if from the ground, not more than a stone's throw from the circle of men around the gold.

Ghostly white, the phantom moved serenely toward the gallows. It was merely a full hand taller than the largest of sheriff's men, not four or five hands taller as the black specter had been.

In the dim moonlight, it did not show arms. Nor a face. A motionless cowl covered its head.

"All saints preserve us!" screamed the voice of the first soldier.

"Advance or you'll lose your heads!"

immediately countered the commander's voice. "Move together or die in the morning!"

After some moments, all eight men began to step slowly forward with swords drawn.

The phantom stopped and waited. It did not speak.

A cloud blotted the moon completely. The men hesitated, then gasped as an eerie glow came from within the pale body of the phantom. Some stumbled backward on the uneven ground.

"Hold, you cowards," came the tense voice of the commander. The retreating men froze.

"A third of the gold to the one who defeats this apparition!" from someone in the pack

Still, the phantom said nothing and held its position.

Finally, just as the cloud began to break away from the moon, the one soldier with the sharpened long sword began a rush at the phantom. "Join me!" he shouted. "Show no fear!"

The point of his outstretched sword had

almost reached the outline of the phantom when a roaring explosion of white filled the soldier's face. The ground rippled for yards in every direction.

"Aaargh!" the soldier screamed, falling sideways as his sword clattered uselessly to the ground.

No man had time to react.

The phantom moaned as it became a giant torch of anger. Flames reached for the soldier on the ground, and he crabbed his way backward, screaming terror.

The other soldiers finally unfroze. They stepped back to huddle in a frightened knot. Each man stared wild-eyed at the flames, which outlined the figure of the phantom. Each man whispered hurried prayers and crossed and recrossed themselves in the anguish of fear.

"A spirit from the depths of hell," one soldier groaned. "Spreading upon us the fires which burn eternally."

As in response, the flames grew more intense, still clearly showing the shape of the phantom. And it said nothing.

The men stood transfixed. Nearly half an hour later, the last flame died abruptly and the phantom collapsed upon itself. The men did not approach.

One soldier finally thought to glance at the gallows. The large bag of gold no longer rested in the center of the wooden structure.

Sir William stirred as a shadow blocked his face from the early morning sun. He had not slept well anyway—the ground was lumpy and cold, and both the pickpocket and mute girl had pressed hard against him to seek warmth during the night.

He blinked open his eyes at a mountain of black which filled the entire sky above him.

"Mother of saints," he said with no emotion. "If you are not the boy Thomas, I am a dead man."

"Your control is admirable," breathed the specter in low rasping tones. "It makes you a valuable man."

With a slight grunt, Sir William sat upright. His movement woke the pickpocket and the girl.

Her hands flew to her mouth, and she bit her knuckles in terror. The pickpocket tried to speak, but no sound came from his mouth.

"Send them down to the stream," the cowled specter said in his horrible voice. "Our conversation will be private."

Neither needed a second invitation to flee, and were far from sight long before the bushes in their way had stopped quivering. Sir William stood and measured himself against the specter's height. His head barely reached the black figure's shoulders.

A twisted grin crossed Sir William's face. "May I?" he asked, motioning at the flowing robe at his waist.

The specter nodded.

Sir William pulled back the robe. He snorted exasperated disbelief. "Stilts indeed."

Thomas leaned forward, and as the stilts fell free, hopped lightly to the ground. He peeled back the ominous cowl. Strapped to his face was a complicated arrangement of wood and reeds that looked much like a squashed duck's bill.

He loosened the straps. The piece fell into his hands, leaving behind deep red marks across his cheeks.

"Much better," Thomas said in his normal voice. He rubbed his cheeks, then grinned.

In that moment, the knight saw the unlined face of a puppy again—but quickly swore to himself not to forget the puppy had sharp teeth.

The knight shook his head again and gruffened his voice to hide any admiration that might slip through. "And I suppose you can equally explain the fire from your sleeve."

Thomas pulled his sleeves free from his arms to show a long tube running from his wrist up to his armpit. "A pig's bladder," he explained as he raised one arm to show a small balloon of cured leather. "I squeeze—" he brought his elbow down and compressed the bag "—and it forces a fluid through this reed. I simply spark it—" he flicked something quickly with his left hand "—and the spray ignites."

Sir William nodded, simply because he could think of nothing to say.

"Unfortunately," Thomas mumbled as he remembered how helpless he had felt when the old man challenged him in front of the crowd, "it only works once. Then the bag needs refilling."

"The fluid?"

Thomas shook his head. "I need to keep *some* secrets."

"How did you blind those sheriff's men?"

Thomas lifted his other arm to show a small tube of clay strapped to his left wrist. This crucible had a long, tiny neck that pointed almost like a finger.

"Another fluid," Thomas explained. "I sweep my hand and it spews forth. It burns any flesh it touches."

"Another secret, I suppose."

Thomas shrugged. He then said, "I also have the gold. From the gallows. Is that enough proof that I was the one who saved your life?"

"Perhaps. More trickery?"

"*Simple* trickery. Shorter stilts and a white cape around me, supported inside like a tent by a framework of woven branches.

The cape was waxed and oiled. I lit a candle inside, stepped back through a flap, and let it burn itself down. It was enough distraction to sneak to the gallows."

Thomas did not mention the mixture of charcoal, sulfur, and potassium nitrate—which men in later centuries would call gunpowder—that he had exploded in a flash of white to temporarily blind all the sheriff's men of their night vision. It was another secret which might lead to questions about the precious books.

"You think you have great intelligence," the knight observed dryly.

Thomas thought of the endless hours his childhood nurse Sarah had spent coaching him through games of logic, through the painful learning of spoken and written Latin and French, through the intricacies of mathematics. Thomas thought of his greatest treasure—the chest filled with books. But Thomas did not think of his intelligence.

"I have been taught to make the most of what is available," he replied without pride.

The knight sprang forward with blurring swiftness, reaching behind his back and pulling from between his shoulder blades in one smooth motion a short sword.

Before Thomas could draw a breath, Sir William pinned him to the ground, sword to his throat.

"You are a stupid child," Sir William said coldly. "Not even a fool would disarm himself in the presence of an enemy."

Thomas stared into the knight's eyes.

Sir William pressed the point of the sword into soft flesh. A dot of blood welled up around the razor sharp metal. "Not even a fool would walk five miles into a desolate forest with a king's ransom of gold, and offer himself like a lamb to a man already found guilty of stealing a sacred chalice."

Thomas did not struggle. He merely continued to stare into the knight's eyes.

"And," Sir William grimaced as he pressed harder, "lambs are meant for slaughter."

The dot of blood beneath the blade swelled to a tiny rivulet.

"Cry you for mercy?" Sir William shouted.

Neither gaze wavered as the two stared at each other.

"Blast," Sir William said as he threw sword aside. "I was afraid of this."

He took his knees off Thomas' chest, and stood. Then he leaned forward and grabbed Thomas by the wrist and helped him to his feet. Sir William gravely dusted the dirt off his clothes, then from Thomas.

It was his turn to grin at Thomas. "The least you could have done was proven to be a coward. Now I have no choice."

Thomas waited.

"For saving my life," Sir William said, "you have my service as required. I ask of you, however, to free me as soon as possible, for I have urgent business of mine."

"Agreed," Thomas said. He refrained from showing a secret smile. Yes, only a fool would have brought a king's ransom of gold to a stranger. The knight did not need to know that Thomas had hidden the bulk of the gold among his precious books. And, of course, the knight did not need to know of the books.

In the quiet of the woods, they clasped hands to seal the arrangement. Left hand over left hand, then right hand over right hand.

"Now what service do you want of me that was so important to risk your life as first a specter, then a midnight phantom?" Sir William asked.

Thomas let out a deep breath. "We shall conquer a kingdom," he said. "It is known as Magnus."

THOMAS
The Dungeon of Doom

The wind, as it always did in the moors, blew strong. Above them, blue sky patched with high clouds. Sir William led the way along a narrow path cutting through the low patches of heather. They had traveled across the tops of the moors. The valley bottoms offered too much cover for ambushing bandits, an event all too common.

Behind the knight, Thomas and Tiny John—as they now called the always-grinning pickpocket—followed closely. The mute girl, farther back, meandered her way in pursuit, stopping often to pluck a yellow flower from the gorse or to stare at the sky.

When their journey had begun, the knight had not been cruel-hearted enough to force those two not to follow. Thomas, of course, had his own silent reasons for allowing the girl and the pickpocket to remain. *Take them with you. It will guarantee you a safe journey to Magnus*—Thomas remembered the old man's whisper each time he looked back at the girl.

But, distracting as the mystery in her face could be, Thomas had other matters to occupy his mind.

"Where *is* Magnus," Thomas spat out the words at the endless valley.

Sir William sighed. "Three days of hard travel. Three days of rough cold meals, and nothing but silence from you. *Now* you dance like a child waiting the Feast of May Day." He paused to wipe sweat from his forehead. "With the impossible task you have set for us, I should think you would be in no hurry to arrive at Magnus."

"It's far from impossible," Thomas said. As if to confirm it, he shifted the bundle packed across his shoulders. *Such simple material inside, but enough to conquer a kingdom.*

The knight did not disguise his snort of disbelief. "We are not much of an army.

Only in fantasies do two people find a way to overcome an army within a castle."

"I have the way," Thomas replied. *Given to me by the nurse who served as both mother and father before her death.*

"Thomas, you are almost a man," Sir William said with exaggerated patience. "You must see the world as it is. Castles are designed to stop armies of a thousand. Soldiers are trained to kill."

"Delivered on the wings of an angel, he shall free us from oppression," Thomas said.

Sir William squinted. "Make sense!"

Thomas smiled. *How many times had Sarah made him repeat the plan? How many times had Sarah promised it would only take one fighting man to win the kingdom?*

"There is a legend within Magnus," Thomas said. "'Delivered on the wings of an angel, he shall free us from oppression.' I have been told each villager repeats that promise nightly during prayers. It will take no army to win the battle."

Sir William did not interrupt the rustling of the waving heather for some time. The young man spoke with such conviction.

"You presume much," Sir William finally said, in a gentler voice that did not suggest mockery. "Is there oppression within Magnus? And where do you propose to find an angel?"

Thomas plucked a long stem of grass and nibbled the soft, yellowed end. "I know well of the oppression..." He paused to think of a way to phrase it. "It was told to me by someone who escaped from there. She was like a mother and a father. In fact, I believe my parents had arranged to send her with me when they knew the pox had taken them and there was no relief from the dread disease."

He pulled the grass from his mouth and stared into Sir William's eyes. "Her name was Sarah. She was my teacher and my friend at the abbey. The monks endured her presence only because it was stipulated with the money my parents had left for my upkeep. She taught me to read and write—"

Sir William shook his head in amazement. He should have guessed. "Latin?"

"And French," Thomas confirmed. He said nothing about the necessity of reading because of the books in a chest hidden in a now faraway valley. "Sarah told me it was the language of the nobles and that I would need it when..."

"When?"

"When I took over as Lord of Magnus."

"You sound so certain," Sir William said. "What right have you to take this manor and castle by force?"

"The same right," Thomas said, suddenly cold with anger, "that the present lord had when he took it from Sarah's parents."

Chapter Eleven ~ Part Two

During the next half hour of walking, Thomas only asked one question to break the noise of the wind across the heather. He asked it repeatedly, "Where is Magnus?"

The knight remained in front, seeing no need to answer. The girl still trailed them. Only Tiny John showed enthusiasm, as if they were on an adventure.

"Let me get on the man's shoulders!" Tiny John finally piped in response to the question. "I'll get a good see from there."

Sir William groaned. "I feel like enough of a packhorse without my steed." A cloud of anger passed his face. "First to be arrested falsely for a chalice I didn't steal. But to lose my horse and armor to those scoundrels..."

He caught the anxiety that Thomas betrayed by chewing his lower lip. The knight sighed, a habit that he noticed he'd begun since meeting Thomas.

"Tiny John, get on my shoulders, then." Sir William shook his forefinger hard at the imp. "*Without* taking a farthing from my pockets. I've had enough trouble with you already."

Tiny John only widened his eternal grin and waved a locket and chain at Sir William, who felt his own neck to reassure himself.

"It's the girl's," Thomas said. "Tiny John took it from her this morning. I didn't have the heart to make him give it back yet. And she hasn't noticed anything all day..."

Sir William kept his face straight. *The only reason Thomas would have overseen the theft was because he spent so much time glancing at the girl,* he thought. *It was almost as if she had riveted his heart, and without a word between them.*

Tiny John tossed the locket to the knight. "A peculiar symbol," Sir William mumbled. "Nothing I've seen before."

Tiny John did not give him time to finish wondering. He darted to the knight's back, then scrambled upward to his broad shoulders, and shaded his eyes with his left hand to peer northeast into the widening valley.

Tiny John whistled. "I've caught the spires! Far, far off! But we can make it by eventide."

"Only if I carry you, urchin," Sir William grunted. "And already you're far too heavy for a knight in his fortieth year."

Tiny John dropped to the ground lightly and kept pointing. "That way, Thomas!" he said. "I'm sure I saw the castle that way!"

Thomas said nothing. It was obvious by his eyes that he was mesmerized in thought.

Sir William glanced at the girl, still several hundred yards back. "Rejoin our silent friend," he told Tiny John as he handed him the thin chain and locket. "Return this to her. We will do our best to reach Magnus before nightfall."

❦

Tiny John had been right. With the easy downhill walk, it took them less than four hours to reach the final crest, which over-looked the castle of Magnus. The bells inside the walls surrounding the castle rang to celebrate the church service of *none*—which meant three p.m.—only a few miles before that crest.

They paused at the crest. Not in need of rest. More to comprehend Magnus as it stretched out before them.

"All saints preserve us," breathed Sir William in awe, "Our mission is surely one of suicide."

Even Thomas faltered. "The army—I have been told—is not large."

Sir William laughed a strained whisper. "Why maintain an army when you have a fortress like *that*." He spread out his arms to indicate the situation. "From afar, I wondered about the wisdom of a castle which did not take advantage of height to survey the valley. Now I understand. A force as large as one thousand might be useless in attack against Magnus."

The valley around Magnus differed little from those they had been seeing for the previous three days. The hills were steeper, perhaps, but the grass and woods in the valley bottom were equally rich, and dotted with sheep and cattle.

There were two differences. One, Thomas could see no farmers' huts anywhere in the valley. Two, there was the water.

Magnus stood on an island in the center of a small lake. High, thick stone walls ringed the entire island and protected the village inside.

The keep of the castle—home of the reigning lord of Magnus—rose high above the walls, but safely far inside and away from the reach of even the strongest catapults.

At the north end, a narrow finger of land reached the island. Just before the castle walls, however, it was broken by a drawbridge no wider than a horse's cart. Even if an army managed to reach the lowered drawbridge, soldiers would only be able to cross three of four abreast—easy targets from archers on the walls above.

Water, of course, was available in almost infinite amounts. Lack of food, then, might be the castle's only weak point, because siege was obviously the only way to attack Magnus. With the foresight to store dry foods, the reigning lord of Magnus would never suffer defeat.

For several minutes, Thomas could only stare at his impossible task. He forced himself to remember and believe the plan given him by Sarah.

He hoped the doubt in his heart would not reach his words. Moor wind carried each one clearly to the knight. "If it is so obvious to a military man like you that a host of armies cannot take Magnus by force from the outside," Thomas said, "then the way it *must* be conquered is from the inside."

Although Sir William told himself not to sigh, he did anyway. "That's like saying the only way to fly is to remain in the air. Of course, it can only be conquered from the inside. That's the only way to conquer any castle. Our first question is how to get an army. Then we can face the usual question of how to get that army inside."

Thomas ignored him. "There is something wonderful about a castle this impossible to overcome. Once we have it," Thomas smiled, "it will be that much easier to keep."

He marched forward.

After enough time to hide the bundle he had carried for three days, Thomas returned to the others hidden in the trees near the north end of the lake.

"I think," Sir William said as a greeting, "it would serve us well to hide any signs of my trade."

"Can it be that serious?" Thomas asked.

"More than you might imagine. Whatever your nurse taught you in that forsaken abbey could not have shown you how drastically the earls and lords of any land guard against any threats to their power."

"But against a single man? I would have thought rebellion in the form of a peasant army or even a gathering of knights—"

Sir William shook his head grimly and lowered his voice. "Now is not the time to explain. Let it suffice to say that serfs and peasants have so little training and so little weaponry that they are considered harmless. So harmless that one man with training or weapons can rise far above an entire village in potential for danger."

On foot without lance or horse, without

full armor or following squire to tend his gear, Sir William did not at first glance appear to be a knight. After the rescue at the gallows, the sheriff's men had given back to him only his chain mail and one of his swords. Sun's disappearance or not, no sheriff would dare risk an earl's displeasure by sending a knight with unknown allegiance forth into the land with full fighting gear.

He smiled to himself a tight smile of irony. As much as he had regretted the absence of the rest of his equipment, this was one moment he did not mind to be without. A knight who did not declare himself as such when approaching the castle of a strange earl or lord could expect immediate death if discovered.

Even without his usual full range of war gear, however, Sir William still did not feel safe from notice. He knew that the guards at the gate would be trained to search for the faintest of military indications of any approaching stranger.

The chain mail covering Sir William's belly, of course, was an immediate giveaway should it be found. Sir William drew his shirt tighter and checked for any gaps, which might betray the finely worked iron mesh. To be totally risk free, he should have abandoned the chain mail miles before the castle. But then he would have been as vulnerable to the thrust of a sword as a piglet before slaughter.

His own short sword—of the type favorite for in-close combat since the time of the mighty Roman legions—hung in a scabbard tightly bound to his back between his shoulder blades. Once again, it would have been much safer to leave the sword behind, but next to impossible to find a weapon inside the castle walls. Sir William would have to risk being searched.

And he could lessen the chances of search.

Sir William dropped his cloak onto the ground. He wrapped himself again without shaking it clean. He smudged dirt into his face, and ran debris into his hair.

"Show no surprise when I become a craven fool," Sir William warned. He turned to Tiny John with a savage glare. "Stay behind and hold the girl's hand. One word, urchin, and you'll lose both your hands."

Tiny John gulped and nodded.

The four of them—a full grown man, a half grown man, a small boy, and a mute girl—made a strange procession as they moved from the cover of the trees to the final approach into Magnus.

o castle is stronger than its weakest part," Sir William grumbled as they reached the finger of land that reached to the castle island. "And generally that is that gatehouse entrance. This does not bode well for your mission."

"Expert military advice?" Thomas bantered. Almost within the shadows of the towers of Magnus, he could not be swayed from his high spirits.

Tiny John remained several steps back with the girl, head craned upward to take in the spires. His grin, unlike that of Thomas, was finally dampened by those same cold shadows.

"Not advice. Sober fear," replied Sir William. "Unless a man can swim—" Sir

William snorted "—which is unnatural for any but a fish, the lake is impossibly wide."

"Nobody *swims* across," Thomas argued. "That's why the drawbridge."

"Not swimming *toward* the castle. *Away*. Defenders often force attackers into the water. Those steep banks make it impossible for a man to get out again." Sir William shuddered. "Especially weighed down with the iron of armor."

Sir William pointed farther. "Worse. This road is the only approach to the monster castle, and I've never seen a *barbican* protecting wall which stretches an entire arrow's flight from the drawbridge to the gatehouse. And nearly straight up!" Lined with small stone towers on each side—only small in comparison to the twin towers of the gatehouse itself—thick walls guarded a steep approach to the castle entry.

"If this gives a hint of the defenses, I can only guess at the treacherousness of the gatehouse itself," Sir William said. He opened his mouth to say something, then paused as a new thought struck.

"Not even *vespers*, the sixth hour past noon. Yet this road is as quiet as if it were already dusk. No passersby. No farmers returning from the fields. No craftsmen to, or fro. What magic keeps this castle road so quiet?"

"What does it matter?" Thomas shrugged. "All we need to do is get within the walls as any passing strangers seeking a night's rest. From there, we shall find the weakness of Magnus and complete my plan. It only makes me happier to see how difficult it is to attack. As I have said, once we have this, it only makes it easier for us to keep—"

"Don't be a blind fool," snapped Sir William. "I am bound to you by a vow, but I will not follow you to a certain death. Lords of manors like this have power and wealth beyond your greatest imagination. You think there is no reason he has remained lord since taking it? Inside those walls soldiers jump at his every whim. It is a rule of nature that when men have power, they use it with joy, and also use it mercilessly to keep it."

"Sir William," Thomas said, unperturbed by the knight's sudden anger. "Not once have I given you an indication that I expected you to fight any soldiers. I simply need your military knowledge."

Thomas thought of his books, hidden safely three days to the southwest of them. "With you as adviser, I have ways of using my own powers..."

Sir William checked his still rising anger and rubbed his chin. *Had not, after all, the sun grown to darkness? What powers did this boy possess? And what gave him such confidence?*

"We shall proceed to the gatehouse," Sir William said. "But slowly. I do not like this situation at all."

As they began the journey across the narrow finger of land to the drawbridge, Sir William began to drag one foot, and he worked enough spit into his mouth so that it drooled from his chin.

A huge lattice wall of wood meshed with iron bars hung head high above the first opening past the drawbridge. Each iron bar ended in a gleaming spike.

"Not good," Sir William whispered.

"Someone cares enough to maintain those spikes in deadly order. An indication of how serious they are about security." He motioned his head briefly at the shadows of two men standing against the sunlight at the next gate at the end of the stone corridor that ran between the portals. "All those soldiers beyond need do is release a lever, and those spikes crash down upon us like a hammer of the gods."

Thomas held his breath. The gate remained in place as they passed beneath.

Sir William maintained his low, whispered commentary as he trudged and leaned heavily on Thomas. "Look above and beside. Those slots in the stone are called 'murder-holes.' Designed for spear thrusts, crossbow arrows, or boiling liquids from hidden passages on the other side."

Thomas tried not to wince.

With his dragging foot, the knight tapped a plank as wide as two men imbedded in the stone floor. "It drops to a chute, I'm sure, straight to the dungeon."

The knight took two more slow and weary steps, then paused, as if for rest, just before earshot of the two guards. He spoke

clearly and softly from the side of his
mouth in the dark corridor as he wiped his
face of pretended fatigue.

"Thomas, the outside defenses of this
castle are as fiendish and clever as I've seen.
It does not bode well for any man's chances
on the inside. There is only you and I.
Something impossible like this..." Sir
William hesitated, and without realizing his
action, lightly touched the scar that ran
jaggedly down his cheek "You may still turn
back with honor. And live."

homas felt very young as he stared at the broad shoulders of the first soldier at the gate.

How could he really expect his fantasy to come true?

Night after night, on the straw bed during his waking dreams of glory in the darkness of the abbey, it had seemed so easy. Now, in the harshness of the sunlight and the dust and the noise of the village beyond the stone-faced soldiers, it seemed impossible. Not even the solid presence of Sir William helped.

The guards blocked a narrow entrance cut into the large gate. Dressed in brown, with a wide slash of red doth draped across their massive chests, each stood as straight and as tall as the thick spears they balanced beside them.

"Greetings to you," Sir William said in a hopeful, almost begging tone.

The guards barely grunted to acknowledge the arrival of the newcomers.

Thomas forced himself to look away from the cold eyes of the soldiers. *These men were so fierce, so dominating...*

Suddenly, the guard on the right whirled! He tossed his spear sideways at Sir William!

"Unnnggghh," the knight said weakly. He brought his left hand up in an instinctive and feeble motion to block the spear that clattered across his chest. The effort knocked him back, and Sir William sagged to his knees.

"I beg of you," he moaned as spit dribbled from the side of his mouth. "Show mercy."

The soldier stood over him and studied the dirty cloak as Sir William cowered.

What was this? A knight of the realm whimpering as pitifully as a starving dog?

Thomas could scarcely believe his eyes. No code of knighthood that he knew would permit this. Without honor, a knight was nothing. Even death was preferred to the showing of fear.

Yet, even as Thomas held his breath in horror, a thought nudged the back of his mind. A thought from one of his precious books. A thought written by the greatest general of a faraway land who had lived and fought more than fourteen centuries earlier.

One who wishes to appear to be weak in order to make his enemy arrogant must be extremely strong. Only then can he feign weakness.

Thomas decided that for this unlettered knight to know such wisdom by instinct was truly more amazing than the cowardice he allowed to appear.

Thomas grinned inside. He felt fractionally more confident than he had upon approaching the gate.

Finally, the soldier sneered downward at Sir William. "Mercy indeed. It's obvious you need it. Get up, you craven excuse for a man."

Sir William wobbled back onto his feet. The spit on his chin showed flecks of dirt.

"Lodging for the evening, good sir," the knight pleaded. "We are not thieves, but workers seeking employment."

Sir William fumbled through his leather waist pouch and pulled free two coins. "See, we have money for lodging. We ask no charity of the lord of the manor."

The second soldier laughed with cruelty. "Make sure it is cleaning and slopping you seek. Not begging as it appears."

The first soldier kicked Sir William. "Up. Get inside before we change our minds."

Sir William howled and held his thigh where the soldier's foot had made a sickening thud. He hopped and dragged his way inside the gate without looking back to see if Thomas and the two children followed.

Thomas pushed Tiny John and the girl ahead of him.

Not until they had turned past the first building inside did Sir William stop. He waited and watched Thomas with a proud chin and guarded eyes.

Thomas did not let him speak. "Artfully done," Thomas said quickly before the knight might decide to explain his cowardice. "By using your left hand instead of the right when he threw that spear, you made it impossible for them to guess you are an expert swordsman."

Sir William grinned wide and sudden, as a warmth of loyalty toward the boy surprised him. The grin then faded as Sir William motioned for them to continue walking.

"I like this less and less," he said in a low voice. "When I showed those coins, I expected greed would force the soldiers to demand the normal bribe for our entry. They did not."

Thomas raised a questioning eyebrow.

"Corruption shows weakness, Thomas. We are now inside, and everything points to unconquered strength."

❧

Thomas usually slept lightly. Years of constant awareness in the abbey had taught him to do so. Here, in strange lodgings, with a fortune of gold hidden in his leather pouch, he expected even the slightest shifting of movement would have pulled him from deep slumber.

So it was a surprise for him to discover the girl gone when he woke as first light nudged past the wooden crossbeams of the crude windows high on the dirty stone wall.

Thomas, of course, did not stop to wonder why his first waking thoughts—and his first waking glance—had turned to her. Even if he had not directed more than a dozen words at her over three days.

The knight could have explained with a knowing smile. At least a dozen times each day, Sir William had hidden his amusement to notice Thomas blushing at eye contact with the silent girl. Most of the knight's amusement came from remembering that with approaching manhood came powerful befuddling emotions. Especially when one finally noticed the curve of a girl's smile.

The knight, long past those days himself, and familiar with the ways to make a woman laugh with joy in his presence, had early decided only the girl's poor rags hindered grown men from staring at her now with unhidden admiration. In a few years, he knew, even the coarsest of clothing would not be able to keep that beauty from shining. Much of it came from the mystery of thoughts hidden in a flawless face. The rest, from the grace of her slim body as she moved it effortlessly in a walk that suggested the confidence of royalty.

Yes, the knight had judged each time Thomas blushed, *the girl will become a woman who makes men gladly play the fool for her*. And each time Sir William had made that bittersweet judgment over the last few days, he had also forced away—knowing he was bound by a pledge of gratitude—questions of the fate of a woman who so easily did the same to and for him.

It was the beginning of the fourth day together for Thomas and Sir William. The knight's dream of that same woman was interrupted by the slight scufflings as Thomas rose to his feet.

"She's gone," Thomas blurted.

"She is indeed," Sir William replied sadly, trying to hold the last of his dream.

"We don't even know her name. So many times I wanted to speak, yet..."

"It happens that way."

Silence.

Sir William shook away the visions that had called him in sleep.

Thomas wondered about an ache he couldn't explain.

Tiny John merely sat up, hunched against his knees in his corner position, and grinned at the world.

I'm in Magnus, Thomas thought. *Here with a task that threatens my life, will test everything I have been taught, and demand that I use every power available to me. Yet my mind turns to sadness. How could that have happened simply because of...*

The girl pushed open the door by walking backward through it.

When she turned, the bowls of steaming porridge in her hands gave obvious reason for her method of entry.

She looked shyly at Thomas. For the first time since the gallows, she smiled.

I shall conquer the world, Thomas finished in his mind. *Lead me to the lord of Magnus.*

he walls of Magnus contain no mean village. There must be nearly eight hundred inside the walls," Sir William said. "I'm surprised it has no fame outside this county."

And I'm more surprised, he thought anxiously, *that there was so little traffic on the road during our approach. Towns this size draw people from two, sometimes more, days' travel in all directions.*

He did not voice his worry.

It would not have mattered anyway.

Thomas was too busy staring in all directions to reply. While he had occasionally visited the village nearby the abbey on market days, not once had he arrived at the hour of early morning activity.

Already the clamor in Magnus was at a near frenzy.

"Fresh duck!" a toothless shopkeeper shouted as he dangled it by the feet in one hand, and with the other waved at Thomas. "Still dripping blood! And you'll get the feathers at no charge!"

Thomas smiled politely and followed closer behind the knight. He could only trust Tiny John and the girl would do the same.

Shops crowded the street so badly that the more crooked buildings actually touched roofs where they leaned into each other. Space among the bustling people between the rows of shops was equally difficult to find.

Thomas scanned the buildings for identification. "Apothecary," he mumbled to himself at a colorfully painted sign displaying three gilded pills. He made a note to remember it well. The potions and herbs and medicines inside might be needed on short notice.

He mentally marked the signs of each shop, even as he enjoyed the feeling of a crowd after so much silence in the abbey.

A bush sketched in dark shades—the vintner, or wine shop. Two doors farther along, a horse's head—the harness maker. Then a unicorn—the goldsmith. A white arm with stripes—the surgeon-barber. There was a potter, a skinner. Shoemaker. Beer seller. Baker. A butch—

Butcher. How could he have been so careless.

Thomas grimaced and pulled his foot away from the puddle of sheep's innards that had been thrown into the middle of the street. Butchers did their slaughtering on the spot for customers, and left behind the waste for the swarms of flies which were already forming black patches on nearby filth.

"Where is it we go?" Thomas called to the knight's shoulders which cleared room, step by step, in front of him.

"A stroll," Sir William said shortly. "I have a few questions which simple observation should answer."

They continued. At the end of the first street, they turned left, then left again to follow another crooked street. It took them away from the market crowd, and past narrow and tall houses squeezed tightly together.

The girl caught up to Thomas. He remembered what Sarah had taught him about manners, and quickly moved so that he walked on the outside, to ensure the girl stayed on the inside nearer to the houses. Thus, if a housewife emptied a jug of water or a chamber pot onto the street from the upper stories, Thomas would suffer, not the girl.

She seemed content to stay beside him, glancing over to smile whenever Thomas stared at her for too long.

In contrast, Tiny John burned with energy and scampered in circles around them. First ahead to Sir William, then back to Thomas and the girl.

"Check his pockets," Sir William said without breaking stride. "Make sure they're empty. If that little rogue so much as picks a hair from a villager, all of us are threatened."

Tiny John stuck out his tongue at the knight, but quickly pulled his pockets open to show he'd managed to remain honest.

More walking.

Thomas then sniffed the air with distaste. They were approaching the far edge of the town—the traditional location of tannery because of the terrible smell of curing hides.

Thomas knew the procedure too well. How many times had one of the monks at the abbey ordered him to scrape away hair and skin from the hide of a freshly killed sheep? As many times, he replied to himself, as they had then ordered him to rub it endlessly with the normal amount of cold chicken dung. That ingredient, plus the fermented bran and water which was used to soak hides, made it an awful job.

They walked by the tannery quickly. Thomas felt sympathy as he watched one of the apprentices scraping flesh, mouth open to keep his nostrils as useless as possible.

The street turned sharply, and within a few hundred more paces, they were back within earshot of the market.

"Stay with me," Sir William said. "We need to learn more."

Just before reaching the market area, Sir William held up his hand.

"Thomas," he said with low urgency. "Look around. What strikes you?"

Thomas had a ready reply. "The crippled

beggars. The men with mutilated faces. Far more than one would expect."

The knight's eyes opened wide. He paused. "My mind was on military matters. I had not noticed. Surely the lord of Magnus hasn't..."

Thomas shrugged. "I have been told many stories of the evil here. Mutilation as punishment among those stories." And in his mind, Thomas heard Sarah singing gently: *Delivered on the wings of an angel, he shall free us from oppression.*

Sir William said, "Scan the shop signs. Tell me what's missing."

"Missing?"

The knight only frowned in thought. Thomas began to study the busy scene ahead.

Finally Thomas answered. "I see no blacksmith."

"You speak truth. Why is that significant?"

More waiting. This time, Thomas shook his head in apology.

"Don't bother yourself for missing the answer," Sir William said. "You have not developed your military thinking."

Sir William then pursed his lips sternly as his deep thoughts remained. "Horseshoes and hoes are not the only items a blacksmith will make."

"Swords," Thomas said after a moment. "Blacksmiths also forge swords. Without a blacksmith, there are no weapons. No armor. Whoever controls Magnus takes few chances."

"Well spoken." The knight was impressed. Thomas showed a rare mind. One which grasped simple facts and drew them together for meaning.

Before Sir William could comment further, a small man broke toward them from the fringes of the crowd.

His shoulders were so insignificant, they were nearly invisible under his brown full-length cloak. A tight black hat only emphasized the smallness of his head. His wrinkled cheeks bunched like apples as he smiled.

"Strangers!" he cackled.

Thomas made a move to step around him.

Sir William shook his head at Thomas, then addressed the small, man. "What might be your name, kind man."

"I am Geoffrey. I make candles. Big ones. Little ones. Thick ones. Skinny ones. The finest in the land. Why, the smoke from these candles will wipe from a window with hardly any—"

"Sold." Sir William jammed his single word into the pause that Geoffrey was forced to take for breath.

"Sold?" Geoffrey's confidence wavered at this unexpected surrender. "I've not shown a one. How can you say—"

"Sold," Sir William repeated firmly. He pulled a coin from his pouch. "Maybe even as many as we carry."

He peered past Geoffrey's shoulders. "Where might your shop be?"

Geoffrey opened and closed his mouth, again and again, like a fish gasping for air. He did not take his eyes away from the coin in Sir William's palm.

"My... my shop is away from the market. I only bring enough candles for the morning's sales. I..."

"Lead on, good man," Sir William said cheerfully. "It's a pitiable guide who cannot find his own shop."

"He's a blathering fool," Thomas whispered to Sir William as soon as it was safe. "What do you want from him?"

"Certainly not candles," Sir William whispered from the side of his mouth. "I want a safe location to ask questions."

Thomas could not fault the knight his strategy. Yet must the information come from an empty-headed babbler like the one clearing a path for them through the crowd?

Every five steps or so, Geoffrey rudely pushed people aside—despite his runt-like size in comparison to most men. The spectacle of the resulting arguments proved to be a humorous distraction.

Too much of a distraction.

Otherwise Thomas or Sir William might have observed the three soldiers who followed them from the simple distance of a stone's throw farther back in the crowd.

ust as Thomas began to see clearly the jumble of vats and clay pots in the dimness of the candlemaker's shop, a ghostlike bundle of dirty white cloth rose from a corner and moved toward him.

Thomas brought both of his fists up in reflex, then relaxed as he noticed that the worn shoes at the base of the ghost had very human toes poking through the leather.

He backed away to make room, and the bundle of cloth scurried past, bumping him with a solidness that no ghost could give. Moments later, it squeezed past Tiny John and the girl.

"That's Katherine," Geoffrey the candlemaker said. "Daughter of the previous candlemaker. Ignore her. She's surprised because I've returned early from the market, and she's afraid of people."

Thomas watched her shuffle past a curtain and out of sight in the back of the cramped house.

"The bandages around her head?" Sir William asked.

"It's to keep people from screaming at the sight of her. When she was little—I am told—she reached up and grabbed a pot of hot wax. No mind that she'd been warned a hundred times. No mind at all. She learned the lesson, she did. It poured over her face like water. The foolish child jumped blind into the flame warming the pot. Yes indeed. As bright as a torch she became. And with half the customers standing in your very spot. The business that was lost because of her screaming." The candlemaker waved his hands as if dismissing the importance. "It's a curse she did not die. I was stuck with her as part of the arrangement to take over this shop on the owner's death. Who might marry her now? And I'd get no price for her if she did, that's the truth."

The candlemaker shrugged before moving on to business. "The will of the Lord, I suppose."

Year after year at the orphanage compressed into a single moment for Thomas.

He turned on the candlemaker with a bitterness he did not know he possessed. "How can you say there is a God who permits this? How can you give that girl less pity than a dog?"

"Thomas." Sir William's calm rebuke drew Thomas from his sudden emotion.

"I give her a home," the candlemaker said in a hurried voice. "It's much more than any dog gets. You've seen the beggars and cripples that gather around. She could be cast loose among them."

Thomas told himself he had no right to interfere. "I ask your forgiveness," he said coldly and without a trace of apology. "For a moment, her situation reminded me of someone I once knew."

Thomas did not explain that he meant himself and his lonely aching years as an orphan freak in the abbey. His heart cried for the pain he knew Katherine suffered; yet moments later, his brain sadly told him there was no use in caring. The candlemaker was right. In this town alone, there were dozens of beggars and cripples who had less than Katherine.

Such pain, Thomas added silently to himself, *is all the more reason to be angry at this God those false monks so often proclaimed.*

Thomas spoke to move from the subject. "We came for candles."

Relief brightened the candlemaker's face. "Yes. I'll bring my finest."

He clapped his hands twice.

Immediately Katherine appeared with a wooden box.

"She must earn her keep," Geoffrey said defensively as he glanced at Thomas.

Thomas said nothing. He looked away from the bundled clothes with outstretched arms. The wrap around Katherine's head was stained with age, with slits for her eyes, and was almost caked black around the hole slashed open for her mouth.

"I'll take the entire box," Sir William said. "You've made mention this is not a town for strangers."

"These are my best candles," Geoffrey said. "I'm surprised you don't know the reputation of Magnus."

Much as Sir William wanted information, he knew better than not to barter. There would be no quicker way to raise suspicion than appearing not to care about price.

"Perhaps these are the best candles you have. But compared to London..." Sir William shook his head to reflect doubt. "In London, the name Magnus stirs no fear into the hearts of good citizens."

"I've not been to London," Geoffrey said as wistfulness momentarily sidetracked him. "Few of us ever leave Magnus."

He coughed quickly to hide embarrassment at his ignorance, then grabbed the box from Katherine and shook his head as she cowered and waited for instructions.

Thomas felt a comforting hand on his shoulder, even as he winced to see Katherine's fear. The mute girl had seen the pain on his face and moved beside him. Tiny John also seemed subdued at the horror of Katherine's primitive mask. He clung to the edges of the mute girl's dress.

The three of them stayed in a tight cluster, and Thomas felt a great sadness to know their instinctive joining resulted from the status of outcast they all shared.

"I apprenticed from the best master for miles around, I don't need to see London candles to know these burn as bright as any in the land," Geoffrey said as he forced his voice back to a sales pitch. "And I don't need to see London to know the reputation of Magnus."

"A farthing each dozen," Sir William offered. "And hang this reputation at which you hint of this place."

"Two farthings and no lower," Geoffrey countered. "And strangers as good as you have said less about Magnus and died for it."

Thomas gave the conversation full attention.

"Two farthings for a dozen and a half." Sir William lowered his voice. "And who might be doing the killing?"

Geoffrey shook his head and held out his hand. "The color of your money first. This box holds three dozen candles."

"Four farthings, then. You drive a hard bargain." Sir William counted the coins. "About this fearsome domain..."

Even in the dimness, Thomas could see the eager glint of a born gossip in the candlemaker's eyes.

"A fearsome domain indeed," Geoffrey said. He looked around him, even though he knew every inch of his own shop. "Ever since Richard Mewburn disposed of the proper lord twenty years ago."

"Surely the Earl of York would not permit within his realm such an unlawful occurrence as murder."

"Bah." A wave of pudgy fingers. "That happened twenty years ago. Since, murder seems the least of crimes here in Magnus. The slightest of crimes results in hideous punishment. Men with their ankles crushed for failing to bow to Richard's sheriff. Branded faces for holding back crops— even though the poor are taxed almost to starvation."

Geoffrey lowered his voice. "The Earl of York is paid rich tribute to stay away. It is whispered that some evil blackmail prevented the earl's father from dispensing justice after Magnus fell to its present master."

Katherine gasped. She had not moved since delivering the candles. The first sound of her voice, eerie and muffled from behind the swath of dirty rags around her head, startled Thomas.

"You cannot reveal this to strangers," she protested. "You sentence them to death!"

Geoffrey brought his hand up quickly, as if to strike the girl.

She stepped back quickly, and bumped a table. Two clay candle molds teetered, then fell to the ground and smashed into dust.

"Clumsy wretch!" the candlemaker snarled. He grabbed a thin willow stick from the table beside him, and whipped it across the side of her head.

Had Thomas paused to think, he would have decided it was her complete acceptance of the cruel pain that drove him to action. She did not cry, did not whimper, merely bowed her head and waited for the next blow.

It tore at his heart to see someone so defenseless, and so undeserving of more pain.

The animal had struck her face. What more cruel reminder of her deformity could exist? And how many times had he done it exactly the same?

Holy rage burst inside Thomas.

The candlemaker raised his arm to strike again.

Thomas roared anger and dove across the narrow space between them. He crashed full force into the candlemaker. Both fell with the body blow. Before the candlemaker could react, Thomas pounced on his chest.

Berserk fury possessed Thomas and he grabbed the candlemaker by both ears. He pulled the candlemaker's head inches from the floor and held it. His arms shook as he fought an overpowering urge to dash the candlemaker's head in one savage motion.

"Foul horrid creature," ground Thomas between clenched teeth. "You shall pay dearly for the abuse—"

He did not finish his threat.

Sir William pulled him upward, and during that motion, the unthinkable occurred.

Soldiers burst into the shop.

Had not Sir William been so helpless with both his arms around Thomas, he might have been able to reach between his shoulder blades and pull the sword free.

Instead, less than a second later, three soldiers had him pinned against the wall.

Two other soldiers grabbed Thomas.

"You hail from the abbey at Harland Moor," the soldier said. It was not a question. "Four monks have been found dead there. One by a blow to the head. Three by poisoning."

The soldier grinned evil. "You and your large companion here will hang. One for murder. The other for aiding a murderer in escape."

Chapter Sixteen ~ Part Two

"Jailer!" Sir William shouted at the rusted iron door in frustration. He did not expect an answer. "Two days have passed. Surely the lord of this manor must appear to us soon!"

"Shhhhh!" hissed a quiet man as he hunched in the corner of the cell and pointed at a tiny hole.

Sir William groaned and looked to Thomas for sympathy.

Thomas shrugged and grinned. Under the circumstances there was little else to do.

What light appeared in the cell came from oily torches outside the grated opening in the door. It only took Thomas two large steps to reach from side to side of the clammy stone walls, three steps to reach front and back. It was so cramped, that had the fetters on the walls been used, one from each side could have placed their wrists in manacles. Yet there were three of them in this small space, sharing the bedding of trampled straw that soaked up the wet dungeon filth.

Thomas dug inside his shirt, searched quickly with his fingers, and snorted triumph.

"Found it."

He withdrew his hand, and squeezed the flea between the nails of his thumb and forefinger until he felt a tiny snap.

"Spare those details, Thomas," Sir William said. "We have much greater concerns. If we are able to meet the lord of this manor we can present our case. He will see there is no injustice in the fate of those monks and then release us."

"I should have sent that letter to the mother abbey at Rievaulx," Thomas said, almost absently as he scratched himself again. "Even if it meant drawing notice to ourselves. We might have been spared this."

Sir William did not have to ask which letter. In the two endless days of darkness and solitude—interrupted only by the bowls of porridge shoved between the bars of the grate twice daily—he had learned of Thomas' final day at the abbey, including the letter of evidence against the monks.

"How often must I tell you?" Sir William said with gentleness. "Unless the lord of Magnus learns the monks poisoned themselves, we will hang. Certainly he must appear to accuse us so that we can defend ourselves."

During those final minutes at the abbey, Thomas had guessed rightly, then, that the food provided by the monks had been poisoned. The monks knew Thomas would immediately retrieve the dangerous letter— as he had—and a slow-acting poison would have both killed Thomas and rid them of the letter.

Yet Monk Philip had found courage enough to warn Thomas.

How could Thomas have known that the act would send him to a dungeon.

"The lord of Magnus will never appear," crowed the man in the corner.

"Ho, ho! After two days, the man of silence speaks," Sir William observed. "Have you tired of your scavenging friends?"

"My good fellow, in my time here, I have seen many like you come, then go to the hangman," the man said, unperturbed by Sir William's jesting tone. "I learned early not to befriend any. It proves to be too disappointing."

He gestured at the corner hole with his hands. "These furry creatures which make their visits, however, are not so fickle. They require little food and their gratitude is quite rewarding. And *they* always return."

Thomas shuddered. He did not need a reminder of the noose awaiting him. He also hoped he would not remain so long in the cell that rats would be more attractive than human company. Not when he had the means to conquer Magnus. *If only he could escape—all it would take was one clear night and...*

The man dusted his hands of the last of the bread crumbs he had patiently held in front of the hole.

"You said the lord of Magnus would never appear," Thomas prompted.

The man did not rise from his squatting position. He merely swivelled on the balls of his feet to face them.

"Never. It is obvious you know nothing of Magnus."

His cheeks were rounded like those of a well-stuffed chipmunk. Ears thick and almost flappy. Half-balding forehead, and shaggy hair, which fell from the back of his head to well below his shoulders. Patched clothing as filthy as the straw, which clung to matted and exposed chest hair.

"It is time to introduce myself," he said with a lopsided grin that showed strong teeth. "My name is Waleran."

He stood, shuffled forward, and—although they were all prisoners in the cell—extended his empty right hand in the traditional clasp that symbolized a lack of weapons.

"Generally, visitors hear nothing from me," Waleran said after Sir William and Thomas had shaken hands with him. "Unlike you, they arrive alone and learn to ignore me after several days. Thus, I am allowed my peace. With two of you, however, the constant talking has given me little peace, and finally I am driven to break my silence."

"Two days of waiting shows remarkable patience," Sir William said.

Waleran shrugged. "I have been here ten years. Time means nothing."

Water ticked in a constant drip from the roof of the dungeon cell to the floor.

"Ten years!" Thomas examined him again. Although pale, Waleran seemed in good health.

"You wonder what crime sends a man here?" Waleran replied to the frank stare. "Simply the crime of being a villager in Magnus. My son, you see, went to the fields outside the castle one harvest day. Instead of threshing grain, he departed. London, perhaps. I am held here as hostage until he returns. And I am held as an example."

Sir William frowned. "How are you an example?"

"To the other families in Magnus. As long as I am here, they know the lord is serious in his edict. No man, woman, or child may leave the village, except to work in the fields and return before nightfall."

"That's monstrous!"

Waleran smiled wanly at Thomas. "Indeed. But who is to defy the lord?"

Sir William began pacing the cell. "It is a strange manor, this Magnus. The lord murders its rightful owner, yet the Earl of York does not interfere. Entire families are kept virtual prisoners inside the castle walls, yet the village does not resist."

"Strange, perhaps, but understandable," Waleran said quietly. "You've seen the fortifications of the castle and outside walls. You've seen that the moors around this make it unapproachable by an army of any size. Even a man as powerful as the Earl of York knows it is fruitless to attack. Besides, the lord of this manor is shrewd enough to give no cause for the earl's anger."

Sir William raised an eyebrow.

Now that Waleran had decided to talk, it seemed as if a flood poured forth. "Because the entire village is in vassalage, this manor is extremely wealthy. The lord gives ample homage to the Earl of York in the form of grain, wool, and even gold. Simple, don't you see?"

"I do see," Sir William said thoughtfully. "The Earl of York is bribed not to attack a castle in his kingdom which he could not successfully overcome anyway."

"Yes, yes!" Waleran nodded quickly. "And with enough soldiers within the gates, the villagers are powerless. Those who do leave to till and harvest the fields know they must return each night, or members of their family will be placed in these very cells. Richard Mewburn may be well hated by those inside Magnus, but all are helpless before him."

"What I don't see," Sir William said in the same thoughtful tones, "is why this lord has not appeared to formally accuse us. Strangers that we are, we deserve the justice which is granted anywhere in the land."

Waleran only shook his head. He returned to his corner, found a crumb to hold above the rathole, then squatted in his former position.

Minutes passed, broken only by the never-ending drips of water onto the stone not covered by straw.

Thomas could not stand it any longer. "That is all?" he cried. "You are choosing silence again?"

Waleran craned his head upward and measured his words.

"My silence would be better for you." He sighed heavily. "Remember I am a reluctant messenger."

Sir William thought of the empty road leading into Magnus. Strong premonition told him he did not want to hear the next words.

"Magnus has around it a black silence," Waleran said. "Traders and craftsmen learned long ago they risked freedom and all they owned to visit. Whispers of death keep them away. And for good reason."

Waleran looked back to the hole and spoke as if addressing the wall. "Had there not been convenient charges against you, you would still have found yourselves within this dungeon. There are dark secrets in Magnus. Secrets only hinted to villagers. Secrets which to survive must remain hidden from the entire land."

He paused, and the deadness in his voice spoke chilling truth. "Strangers, once inside these walls, are never permitted to leave."

homas woke with the sour taste of heavy sleep in his mouth. *Fear and worry must be exhausting me,* he decided as he rolled into a sitting position and wiped straw from his face; *the nights pass without dreams.*

And how is a person to mark the passage of time in this dark hole, he muttered in his mind. *No bells to mark the church offices, no sun to mark dawn or nightfall.*

In the unending dull flickering of torches, Thomas could see that Waleran lay huddled motionless on one side of the cell; Sir William snored gently in his corner.

The knight is tired too, Thomas observed. Neither hidden sword nor concealed chain mail seemed to hinder his sleep.

Who is this knight, Thomas asked himself. *A man of honor, he has fulfilled his pledge by entering the castle walls of Magnus. He has become a friend, yet he speaks nothing of his past, nothing of his own quest he once mentioned.*

Thomas suddenly realized something that he had missed in all his previous thoughts about the knight. *Could the man fight with skill?* Certainly, like any knight, he could easily defeat a dozen unarmed and untrained peasants. That assumption had lulled Thomas into a sense of security. But a new question disturbed him. *Was Sir William man enough to fight boldly against other armed and trained men?*

Thomas pondered the sword and chain mail that the knight refused to hide beneath the straw, then decided yes. They had not been searched before being thrown in the dungeon. Sir William could then have removed the uncomfortable chain mail, but chose not to. Any man who would endure discomfort day and night to be constantly prepared for any brief chance at escape would be a man to have as an ally.

Thomas did not slow his thoughts or silent questions. Tiny John, no doubt, could well find a way to survive. *But was the mute girl withstanding the terrors of being alone and friendless in Magnus?* Thomas regretted again not even knowing her name, and let worry fill his hunger-pinched stomach. It had been four days. The girl could not speak. *What work would she find to sustain her? What stranger might treat her with kindness?* Or—Thomas dreaded the thought—*would she simply flee Magnus and disappear from his life forever?*

"Thomas, you scowl as if we have lost all hope."

Thomas blinked himself free from his trance, and answered the knight's easy smile.

"You are awake?"

In the warmth of their growing friendship, Thomas ached to confide in the knight.

There is so much to tell, Sir William. The chest of books, a source of power as great as any in the land. The gold I have concealed in the cave beside them. The bundle outside the castle, the means of winning Magnus. And the promise made at Sarah's deathbed never to reveal these secrets.

Sir William yawned. "Awake, but my mouth is as vile as goat's dung. Even the water from this roof will be better."

With that, Sir William moved beneath one of the eternal drips and opened his mouth wide. After several patient minutes of collecting water, he rinsed and spit into a far corner of the cell.

Waleran unfolded from his motionless huddle and grumbled. "Must you be so noisy? My friends will never venture forth."

Sir William merely yawned again and said, "Precisely."

Before Waleran could retort, the door rattled.

"A visitor," droned the jailer.

"Impossible," Waleran said. "Not once in ten years has a visitor been permitted to—"

The door lurched open, and the jailer's hand appeared briefly as he pushed a stumbling figure inside.

Thomas tried not to stare.

Caked and dirty bandages still suggested mutilated horror. A downcast head and drooped shoulders still projected fear. Yet it was her.

ho is this wretched creature?"
Waleran demanded.

Again, it hit him, the instant fury that
someone so defenseless might suffer
insults. Thomas spun, shoved his palm into
Waleran's chest, and drove him backward
into the filth.

"Another word and you shall pay—"
Thomas began in a low tight voice.

Sir William stepped between the two.
"Thomas..."

Thomas sucked air between gritted teeth
to calm himself as Waleran scrabbled backward into his corner.

"Please do not hurt him," Katherine said
dearly. "To be called 'wretched creature' is

an insult only if I choose to believe it."

Thomas turned to her. She stood waiting, hands behind her back. She was only slightly shorter than he. Her voice, still muffled by the swathed bandages, had a low sweetness.

"I beg of you pardon," Thomas said. It pained him to look at her. Not because she was a freak. But because he remembered his own pain and loneliness. It tore at his heart to imagine how much worse she felt her private agony.

"How is it you are allowed to visit?" Sir William asked.

Katherine's head nodded downward in shyness. "Every day since your capture, I have brought hot meals to the captain of the guards. I have washed his laundry, cleaned his rooms."

"Bribery!" Sir William laughed. "But why?"

Katherine took a small basket from behind her back. "Because of the candle shop. Not once has a person defended me as you did," she answered. "Prisoners here do not fare well. I wished to comfort you."

She pulled the cloth which covered the basket.

Juices flowed in his mouth as Thomas smelled cooked chicken.

Bread. Apples. Chicken. Cheese.

"These luxuries are more than you can afford," Thomas protested.

She ignored him and offered the basket and held it in front of her until finally he accepted.

"I have little time," Katherine said. "If it pleases you, Thomas, I wish to speak alone."

"You know my name," Thomas said as he handed the basket to Sir William.

"Your friend, Tiny John, told me."

Sir William retreated with the basket to a corner to give them privacy.

"Tiny John! He is well?" Thomas whispered.

"As long as he continues to avoid the soldiers. Many of the shopkeepers take delight in helping that rascal. They like to see the soldiers made fools of."

Thomas pictured Tiny John darting from hiding spot to hiding spot, never losing his grin of happiness.

"And the girl?"

Katherine caught the worry in his voice. She drew a quick breath and turned her head away as she spoke. "The girl truly is beautiful. I understand your concern."

Katherine faced him squarely again, but her voice trembled. "She has disappeared. But if you ask, I shall inquire for you and search until she is found."

Thomas silently cursed himself. How little affection must be in this poor girl's life if a few moments of kindness from him, a passing stranger, kindled the devotion she now showed. Here she stood, knowing her hideous face prevented her from competing for more affection. *And while she waits, with the only gifts she can afford, the passing stranger betrays such obvious concern for another with the beauty she will never have. Thoughtless cruelty of the worst type.*

"No. Please do not look for her," Thomas finally croaked his answer. He blocked thoughts of the mute girl, and measured his words carefully. "We might ask instead that you honor us with another visit."

The squaring of her shoulders told him he had answered rightly.

Besides, he consoled himself, *even if Katherine found the mute girl, what good would it accomplish?*

The jailer rapped on the door. "Be quick about leaving."

"Tomorrow," Katherine whispered, "we shall talk of escape."

THOMAS
NIGHT FLIGHT

Thomas again woke to the sour taste of heavy sleep. He did not move for several minutes; instead he stared at the ceiling of the dungeon cell and watched the water drops.

He began going through his never-ending questions again. Katherine's visits during the past week had helped pass time and given hope, but never enough. In her absence, always, he faced his self-imposed questions.

Who is the knight and can he be trusted with all secrets? Was the mute girl alive? Or nearby? Who was the old man? And the most pressing question: With Katherine's help, would their plan for escape succeed?

The water dripped, uncaring of course about the fate of humans beneath.

Water. Thomas swallowed and licked dry lips. *Water.* He swallowed the sour taste of sleep again. This time thoughtfully. *Water.* A new realization startled him into sitting bolt upright.

He ran idea after idea through his mind. Finally, when his plan was complete, he spoke.

"Escape!" he whispered hoarsely.

Sir William muttered from a deep sleep.

"Escape!" Thomas tried again.

Waleran stirred and groaned as he woke. "What's that you say?"

Thomas grinned at Waleran in response, then stepped across the dungeon cell and shook the knight.

"Escape!" He looked over to Waleran. "Yes! I said escape!"

"Back to sleep, you crazed puppy," Sir William said with a thick tongue.

"No. I cannot." Thomas grinned at Waleran, then at the knight. "Seven days from now we shall leave. The girl Katherine has promised to bribe the captain of the guards to leave our door open." True or not, it was the best explanation he could think to offer. Thomas shuddered to think of their fate if Waleran did not believe him.

❧

"You cannot believe in God. Not if you tell me He is a God of love," Thomas insisted in a low voice.

"Why is that, Thomas?" Katherine replied calmly.

Thomas welcomed the sound of her voice. Especially since Sir William had refused to speak since sheathing his sword that morning. Katherine's cheerful sweetness banished the darkness of the dungeon. They had now spent enough time in conversation to regard each other as friends.

Her voice was so expressive that Thomas did not need to read her face to enjoy their discussions. By now, Thomas hardly noticed the covering of bandages around her head.

"It is hard to believe," he said, "when there is so much evidence that He does not love us."

Thomas had had much time to think since morning. He had questions he hardly dared ask Katherine. Questions of escape that he preferred to delay. Moreover, her presence gave such gentle calmness that he wanted to speak of things he had shared with no living soul since the death of his nurse Sarah.

"Nothing in my life," he said with intensity, "shows such a God. My parents were taken from me—killed by pestilence—before I was old enough to remember them. Then Sarah—my nurse, teacher, and only friend—gone before I was eleven years of age."

Thomas struggled to keep his fists unclenched. "Surely if this God of yours existed, He would have been there in the abbey when all human love failed me. He was not. Instead, there was only corruption by the very men pretending to serve Him."

He described his years in the abbey, and the crimes of the four monks.

"And outside of the abbey," he continued. "A land where most people struggle to live day by day, servants to the very few and very wealthy earls and lords. Beggars, cripples, disease, and death. There is nothing good in this life."

"Thomas, Thomas..." Katherine placed a cool hand upon his.

He shook free. "And you," he blurted with anger. "How could you be so cursed if God truly loved..." Then he realized what he was saying.

"I'm sorry," he said in a low voice.

"Do not trouble yourself," Katherine said. "I am accustomed to the covering of my face."

She touched her bandages lightly. "This is not a curse. It is only a burden. After all, our time on earth is so short."

She moved her hand away from the bandages, then held it up to stop Thomas from protesting.

"Think of a magnificent carpet, Thomas. Thousands and thousands of threads, intertwined in a beautiful pattern. No single thread can comprehend the pattern. No single thread can see its purpose. Yet together, they make the glorious entirety."

She continued with controlled passion. "You and I are threads, Thomas. We cannot see God's plan for us. My scars, your loneliness, the beggars' hunger, and the paths of men in peace and war all lead to the completion of God's design."

"How do you know with such certainty?" Thomas almost pleaded, so sure was her voice.

"God grants you peace when you accept Him."

Thomas shook his head slowly. "I wish I could believe." His own voice rose with passion. "Hear this, when I left the abbey, I left God. I shall not return, to Him, nor to the abbey."

His statement left a silence between them.

On the other side of the dungeon, Sir William sat in a slouched position, ignoring them. Waleran squatted in his normal position and waited with bread crumbs for the rats to visit.

The silence between them nearly became uncomfortable. Thomas decided to ask the question he had delayed from fear.

"Tiny John. Did he succeed?" he breathed.

"Yes, Thomas. I have made the arrangements."

Gratitude swept warmth across him. For the first time since entering the cell, she replaced in his heart, for a moment, the silent girl with the beautiful face and the haunting eyes.

"Then it is nearly time," he murmured. "Spread the legend among the villagers. Have them ready for the knight."

Katherine nodded. "When is it," she murmured in return, "that you wish to escape?"

Thomas thought of the seven days he had promised Waleran.

"In six days," Thomas said. "On the eve of the sixth day from now."

n the eve of the sixth day, Thomas recognized the high pitch of Tiny John's voice echoing in the dungeon hallways long before he could understand the words.

Sir William stopped his silent pacing. "That's—"

"Our pickpocket friend," Thomas finished.

The knight squinted and opened his mouth to ask a question, but was interrupted by the clanging of a key into the cell door.

"Horrid fiend!" the guard shouted. "I hope they tear you into pieces!"

A bleeding hand shoved Tiny John into the cell. He stumbled, but did not fall. The door slammed shut.

Tiny John surveyed his new home with his hands on his hips and grinned. "Barely nicked him, I did," Tiny John explained. "If only my teeth were bigger, I'd have bitten those fingers clean through."

Sir William shook his head in mock disgust.

Waleran moved closer, not bothering to hide a puzzled expression. "Who are you? And what did that soldier mean, 'I hope they tear you to pieces'?"

"I'm John the potter's son. Some say I'm a pickpocket. But don't believe everything you hear."

"But this tearing to pieces..."

"Oh, that." Tiny John waved away the question. "He was right upset, he was. Losing a chunk of his finger and all." Tiny John paused to elaborately spit his mouth clean, then grinned. "I begged him not to throw me in this cell. Told him these two—" Tiny John gestured at Thomas and Sir William "—were unforgiving about some jewelry I'd lifted from them and that I was sure to be killed if he threw me in the same den."

Waleran scowled irritation. "These two would kill you?"

"Of course not," Tiny John said in amazement at Waleran's stupidity. "But how else could I make sure the guard would put me among my friends?"

Waleran sighed.

Tiny John did not notice. He continued in the same cheery voice. "I'm here now, Thomas. Right at eventide as requested. 'Twas no easy task running slow enough for the soldiers to catch me. Especially with so many of my village friends trying to help me escape."

"Right at eventide as requested?" Waleran repeated. He looked to Thomas for help. "He wanted to be captured?"

Thomas scratched his ear with casualness. "I promised him he would be out tonight."

"Tonight? But the escape is tomorrow!" Waleran blurted.

Thomas ignored that and placed both his hands on Tiny John's shoulders. "The villagers expect an angel?"

"Some believe. Some don't. But all wait for tonight."

"Angel?" Waleran interjected. "Tonight?"

Thomas did not remove his glance from

Tiny John's face. "And Katherine has spread word among the villagers?"

"They wait for angels," Tiny John said. "No other legend could prepare them so. And they wait for Sir William."

"Angels?" Waleran almost stamped the ground in frustration.

Thomas removed his hands from the boy's shoulders. "Well done, Tiny John." Then he faced Waleran. "Yes. Angels. Surely as one born in Magnus you recall the legend?"

Waleran opened his mouth and snapped it shut.

Sir William was quick to notice.

"Thomas," he said sharply. "What is it you know about this man?"

Waleran edged away from them both.

Thomas replied with a question. "Do you not think it strange that one who claims to have been in this cell ten years remains so strong and healthy?"

"The rats," Waleran said quickly. "They provide nourishment when I tire of their friendship."

"Draw your sword, please, Sir William," Thomas continued in a calm tone. "If this man opens his mouth to speak again, remove his head. The guards must not hear him shout for help."

The sword had been hidden since the beginning. Yet with almost magical swiftness, Sir William reached back between his shoulder blades and pulled the weapon free. An instant later Waleran felt the prick of a sword blade pushing the soft skin of his throat.

"Explain," Sir William told Thomas in a quiet voice. "I do not care to threaten innocent men."

"Waleran is a spy," Thomas said. "Each night, as we lay in drugged sleep, he leaves the cell and reports to his master."

"Drugged sleep."

"Drugged sleep," Thomas repeated. He thought of the morning he had licked his dry lips and stared at the ceiling. "I believe it is a potion placed into our water each night at supper."

"That explains why you asked me not to drink tonight."

Thomas nodded. "Also, these fetters. I began to wonder why we were not manacled to the walls, as is custom. But Waleran needed to have freedom of movement. We would have suspected too much if we were bound in iron and he were not."

Sir William added pressure to the sword point. "Is the accusation true? Are you a spy?"

Waleran did not reply.

"Answer enough." Sir William held his sword steady and gazed thoughtfully at Waleran. "The foul taste as I woke. The dreamless nights. How I did not suspect..."

"It took me some time too," Thomas said. He glanced at the ceiling as if thanking the drips of water that had triggered his suspicion. "Do your arms tire, Sir William?"

"Of holding a sword to this scum's throat? I think not."

"Please. Let me sit," Waleran suggested nervously. His Adam's apple bobbed against the sword point. "If the sword slips..."

Sir William nodded. "Sit then. But so much as draw a deep breath and you shall be dead."

Waleran burrowed into the straw.

Sir William did not remove his eyes from Waleran's face. "Thomas, Tiny John said we would escape tonight. Yet nearly a week ago..."

"...I announced it would happen tomorrow."

"You knew then that Waleran was a spy?"

"I suspected as much. That night, I poured my water into the straw and pretended sleep. Shortly after, Waleran answered a soft knock on the door, and departed. He returned many hours later."

"Does the lord of Magnus believe we escape tomorrow?" Sir William asked with deceptive calm. His eyes had not wavered from Waleran's face.

"You expect me to reply"

Sir William brought his sword point up again. "These are your choices. You answer to me, and merely risk punishment from him. Or you refuse to answer to me, at the certainty of immediate death. After all, I stand to lose nothing by slaying you."

"Yes," came the quick reply. "He intended to arrest Katherine tomorrow."

"Why were you placed here as a spy?" Sir William asked. "Why would the lord of

Magnus think Thomas and I were important enough to need watching in this cell. I
came in as a beggar, and Thomas as—"

"*And why were you placed here ahead of
our arrest?*" Thomas asked as a sudden new
thought shocked him.

The answer came, as Thomas feared.

"Your arrival—and mission—was expected."

Chapter Twenty-One ~ Part Three

The old man at the gallows!

There was no other way possible for anyone in Magnus to know!

Thomas almost swayed as he fought the rush of excited fear that swept him. *Why help Thomas and the knight escape, only to imprison them at Magnus? Waleran might hold the answer!*

"Tell me who foretold our arrival!" he said in a voice hoarsened by urgency. "And where he is now!"

Waleran shrugged and continued his eerie smile. "I am simply a spy. I only know there are many dark secrets in Magnus."

Sir William glowered and rested the blade of his sword against Waleran's throat.

"Explain yourself."

"That is all I will reveal. Death itself is a more attractive alternative."

Thomas felt chilled. Dark secrets of Magnus? Then he damped his jaw. The only magic in any kingdom was the power held by its lord. And if the moor winds continued to blow, morning would find him holding that power...

"Ignore his blathering," Thomas said. Time was too short. "Sir William, there is much I need to tell you before we leave this cell tonight."

Waleran giggled. "You persist in believing you might leave?"

Thomas nodded at Tiny John.

Tiny John grinned white from a dirt smudged face and pulled from his coat a large key.

"Pickpockets do have their uses," Thomas said.

Sir William frowned. "Any moment the guard will discover it missing and return!"

"Not likely," Thomas said. "Just as Katherine instructed, Tiny John lifted it three days ago when the guard strolled through the marketplace. Katherine waited at the candle shop, then made a wax impression of it, so that Tiny John could return it within minutes. What you now see is a duplicate."

Sir William began to grin as widely as Tiny John, then stopped abruptly. "How do you propose we silence this spy. We have no rope. No gag. As soon as we leave the cell, he'll call for help."

Thomas smiled. "He should sleep soon. I switched cups during supper. Waleran drank the drugged water intended for me."

They encountered the first guard within ten heartbeats of easing themselves from the dungeon cell.

Startled, he stepped backward and placed a hand on the hilt of his sword.

Sir William was faster. Much faster.

Before the guard could flinch, Sir William's sword point pinned his chest against the wall. The guard dropped his hand and waited.

"Run him through!" Tiny John urged.

"Spare his life," Thomas said in a voice which allowed no argument.

"Thomas, I'm not fond of killing people. Believe me. Yet this man has been trained to do the same to us. At the very least, he will sound alarm."

Even in the yellow light cast by smoking torches, the man's fear was obvious by sweat, which rolled down his face.

"You have children?" Thomas asked.

The guard nodded.

"Spare him," Thomas repeated. "I would wish a fatherless life on no one."

Sir William shrugged. Then in a swift motion, he crashed his free fist into the guard's jaw. The guard groaned once, then sagged.

"We'll drag him back into our cell," Thomas instructed. Then he spoke to Tiny John through a smile that robbed his words of rebuke. "This isn't a game, you scamp. Would *you* care to have a sword through your chest?"

Tiny John squinted in thought. "Perhaps not."

Thomas laughed. "Get on with helping us."

Within moments, they left the guard as motionless as a sack of apples beside the snoring Waleran.

Ten minutes later, they reached, undetected, the cool night air and the low mur-

mur of a village settling at the end of an evening.

Thomas smiled at the wind that tugged at his hair.

Sigmund Brouwer

Chapter Twenty-Two ~ Part Three

In the early evening darkness outside the castle walls, Thomas forced away
his fear.

Planning in the idle hours, he told himself,
is much too easy. In grand thoughts and
wonderful schemes, you never consider the
terror of avoiding guards on the battle-
ments and dropping down by rope into a
lake filled with black water.

He shivered in his dampness.

Katherine must be here. Or all is lost.

*Sir William must rally the village people. Or
all is lost.*

The winds must hold. Or all is lost.

Thomas shook his head angrily. *Cast not
your thoughts toward the fears,* Sarah's

patient voice echoed in his memory, *but focus on your wishes.*

At that, Thomas had to grin at the moonlight.

"I want to fly like an angel," he whispered. "Carry me high and far, wind."

As if reading his mind, the wind grew. But with it, his cold beneath the wet clothing.

Five more minutes, he told himself. *If Katherine doesn't appear within five minutes, then I'll call out.*

He counted to mark time as he walked. *The winds blow from the north,* Katherine had said. *Once you reach the open moors, mark the highest point of the hills against the horizon and move toward it. I shall appear.*

With no warning, she did.

"You have retrieved your bundle?" she whispered.

"Yes. Undisturbed. Everything still remains in it."

"Then wrap this around you."

With gratitude, Thomas slipped into a rough wool blanket.

"I've also brought you dry clothing," she said.

Without thinking, Thomas drew her into the blanket, hugged her, and kissed lightly the bandage at her forehead. It surprised him as much as her, and she pulled back awkwardly.

"I'm sorry," he said. "It's just that—"

"Please, dress quickly. Time is short."

Thomas removed his shirt and trousers with numbed fingers. The wind cut his bare skin, but within moments he was fully dressed. Immediately, his skin began to glow with renewed warmth.

"When I am lord," he promised, "you shall have your heart's desire."

"You do not know my heart's desire," she whispered so softly that her words were lost in the wind.

Thomas would not have heard anyway. He was scrambling forward, searching for the sheets and wooden rods he had removed from his bundle. The moonlight aided him.

"I did this as a young child to pass time after my nurse died." Thomas spoke as he worked. This far from the castle walls—several hundred yards—there was no danger in being overheard by a night watchman. "But I confess, it was on a smaller scale."

He tied two rods together at one end, then propped and tied a cross member halfway down, so that the large frame formed an "A."

"However, I have no fear of this failing." He did, of course, but showing that fear to Katherine would not help. "In a strange land, far, far away, it is a custom for men to build one of these to test the gods for omens before setting sail to voyage."

"How is it you know of these things" Katherine stood beside him, handing him string and knives and wax as requested.

Surely there is no harm in telling her, Thomas asked of his long-dead Sarah. *I will not mention the books, only what I learned as a child.*

"You must vow to tell no person." Thomas waited until she nodded. "What I am building comes from the land known as Cathay."

"Cathay! That is at the end of the world!"

Thomas nodded. His hands remained in constant motion. He tested the frame. Satisfied, he moved it to a sheet of cloth, spread flat across the grass.

"It is a land with many marvels," he said

as if he had not paused. "The people there know much of science and medicine. I expect they would be called wizards here."

"'Tis wondrous strange," Katherine breathed.

Thomas nodded. "Their secrets enabled me to win the services of a knight. And now, through the legend of Magnus, a kingdom."

He kneeled beside the frame. "Needle and thread," he called.

Instantly, she placed it in his hands. He began to weave the sheet to the frame. For the next hour, he concentrated on his task, and did not speak.

In equal silence, Katherine placed more thread in his hands as required. The moonlight, bright enough to cast their shadows across their work, hastened their task.

Finally, Thomas stood, and arched his back to relieve the strain. He took the structure and set it upright. The wind nearly snatched it from his hands, and he dropped it again.

Satisfied, he surveyed it where it lay on the ground. As wide as a cart, and as high as a doorway.

He found the loose end of the twine, and tied it to the middle of the crossbar.

There still remained the sewing of bonds that would attach him to the structure. And after that, the flight.

Katherine interrupted his thoughts. Her voice quavered. "You are certain the men of Cathay used such a thing?"

Thomas was glad to speak of what he knew from the books. It took his thoughts from his fears.

He kept his hands busy as he replied. "There was a man from Italy named Marco Polo," he began. "He spent a third of a lifetime living among the people of Cathay." Thomas remembered how he had savored every word of each book, how each page in the dry coolness of the cave had eased the pain of daily living at the abbey. Strange customs and strange men in strange lands.

"This Marco Polo recorded many things. Among them, the custom of sending a man aloft in the winds before a ship sailed from shore. If the man flew, the voyage would be safe. If the man did not stay in the air, the voyage was delayed."

Katherine spoke quickly. "You tell me

that there were times it did not stay in the air."

"Tonight will not be one of them," Thomas vowed. "Too much has happened to bring me this far."

"Then it is God's will that you triumph," Katherine replied.

For the first time since Sarah's death, Thomas permitted a crack in his determined wall of disbelief.

"If that is indeed truth, begin a prayer," he said, then paused. "Begin it from both of us."

❦

The winds held steady.

Thomas ignored the cold as he raced to final readiness.

Would this daring attempt to fly succeed? *Or will my endless dreams and plans and preparations at the abbey end here with my death.*

He tied leather shoulder straps to the cross members of the structure, and another wide leather band that would secure his legs.

Do not think of failure.

He drove a peg into the ground with the hammer that Katherine had smuggled out earlier.

My death here would be of no matter. Should I fail, life will not be important to me. I will never have a chance like this again.

To the peg, he attached one end of a roll of twine, the last object from his bundle.

Do not think of failure.

The other end of twine he tied to a belt of leather around his waist. Between both ends, the remaining twine was rolled neatly on a large spool. Small knots every three feet thickened the twine.

Will the knight be inside waiting with the new army? Or—do not consider the results— has he been captured already?

Thomas looped the handles of a small, heavy bag around his neck. The cord of the bag bit fiercely into his skin and brought water to his eyes.

Do not think of failure.

Finally, he slipped his hands into crudely sewn gloves of heavy leather.

Will the winds be strong enough? Katherine, pray hard for me.

"I will lay down on this," he said. "Attach the straps around my shoulder. That will leave me movement with my arms. When I am ready, please help me to my feet. Then stand aside. The wind should do the rest."

Moving onto his back relieved some of the pressure of the cords around his neck. Thomas fastened himself securely and took a deep breath.

You have dreamed long enough of this moment. Sarah promised you again and again that this kite was the only way to win Magnus. Wait no longer.

"I am ready."

Katherine reached for his outstretched hand. She braced herself, then heaved backward. Thomas lurched to his feet with the huge kite on his back

"Wings of an angel," Katherine breathed in awe.

Chapter Twenty-Three ~ Part Three

mmediately, the wind snatched at Thomas. He grabbed the twine where it was secured to the peg. It took all his strength to hold to the ground.

"Thomas!" Katherine pointed behind him at the castle. "Soldiers! At the gate!"

He could not turn to see. That was the worst of it. He was bound to a kite that would only let him see into the wind—not where it took him, leaving him driven at a brutally high and hard castle wall, which was impossible to watch during his approach.

Two hundred carefully paced steps to reach the walls. Would that give him enough time to soar out of reach?

The wind screamed at the sail on his back

"Flee, Katherine! Away from the castle. Rejoin me tomorrow!"

She shook her head. "Go! God be with you!" With that, she pushed him, and a gust of wind pulled the twine through his hands.

Airborne!

In the next frenzied seconds, Thomas could not give himself the luxury of worrying about the approaching soldiers. The kite picked up momentum so quickly that twine sang through his fingers. Even through heavy leather gloves, Thomas felt the heat.

The moon cast his shadow on the ground, and from his height it appeared like a huge darting bat. The soldiers below him shouted and pointed upward.

He dismissed any joy in this sudden flight. He forced the soldiers from his mind. Instead, Thomas concentrated sharply on counting each knot, his only measure of passing distance. His mind became a blur of numbers. He reached one hundred once, then began over. At eighty again, he clutched hard and the kite swooped upward even more sharply. His fingers froze.

Katherine!

Facing into the wind, Thomas could not see the castle wall, and he saw behind him that the same moon which cut such clear black shadows also showed too clearly that the soldiers had reached Katherine.

Why had she not fled?

Thomas understood immediately.

She protected the peg!

Katherine had grabbed one of the remaining sticks of wood to advance on the soldiers. Once the soldiers reached it, a single slash of sword would sever Thomas from the ground. She knew it. The soldiers, if they did not know it now, would almost immediately upon reaching the peg.

Thomas wailed. *Why had he not told her the twine was needed only briefly?*

"Flee!" he screamed to her. But his words were lost to the wind.

Thomas tore his eyes from the scene below. There was nothing he could do now for Katherine except get over the castle walls on his wings of an angel. He ached to see behind him. How far from the castle walls? He only knew he was not high enough yet to get over the rough stone.

He willed his fingers to release the cord. Eighty-one. Eighty-two. Eighty-three...

A scream pierced the darkness. Soldiers had reached Katherine.

Concentrate!

At ninety-nine, he stopped the unraveling by swiftly lashing the twine around his wrist in two loops. It felt as if the sudden yank of rope tore his hand loose. With his other hand, he fumbled with the sack at his neck, and pulled free its contents, a heavy grappling hook attached to another bundle of twine. Thomas dropped it, knowing there was enough twine for the hook to reach the ground.

Without the extra weight of the grapple, the kite bobbed upward, high enough to clear the castle wall.

At the same time, the tremendous pressure on his lashed wrist ceased.

The rope at the peg has been cut! Katherine!

"Please, God. Be with us now!" Thomas cried into the black wind.

The grappling hook hit the surface of the drawbridge and bounced upward as the wind took the kite.

Savagely, with all the anger he wanted to direct at the soldiers back with Katherine, Thomas wrapped his fingers around the twine which unraveled from the sack around his neck.

"Please, God. Let it hold!"

The grapple hopped upward again, and clacked against the wall of gate before spinning away.

By then, Thomas was over the walls and in sight of anyone within Magnus.

A great shout arose to meet him. Sir William *had* gathered the army!

Clank. The grapple's first bounce against the lower part of the walls.

Thomas held his breath.

The kite tore upward so quickly that barely any wall remained between the grapple and the night sky. If it did not catch, the wings of an angel would carry Thomas far, far away from Magnus. Without Thomas there, Sir William's army would scurry homeward. Never would Magnus be freed from...

Thud.

Despite all the strength he possessed, twine spun through his gloves from the sudden lurch of kite against wind as the grapple dug into the top of the castle wall.

The shout of people below him grew louder.

Thomas still did not dare look downward.

He fought the twine to a standstill, then looped it around his waist belt. Then, and only then, did he survey Magnus.

The kite hung as high as the highest tower. Suspended as it was against the moon, people gathered below could only see the outspread wings of white.

They roared. *"Delivered on the wings of an angel, he shall free us from oppression! Delivered on the wings of an angel, he shall free us from oppression!"*

Thomas nearly wept with relief. He pulled his crude gloves free, and tucked them into the remaining coils of twine in the sack around his neck

"Delivered on the wings of an angel, he shall free us from oppression!"

Thomas could see them all armed with hoes, pitchforks; protected by rough shields of tabletops, helmets of pots. As they shouted, they pumped their hands upward in defiance.

That was the secret to conquering Magnus. Not to find a way to bring an army into it. *But to form one from people already inside*. One knight to lead them. One angel to inspire them.

"Delivered on the wings of an angel, he shall free us from oppression!"

The roar of their noise filled the sky. There were enough to pack the market space and spill into the alleys. Thomas could see no soldiers foolish enough to approach the roiling crowd.

"Delivered on the wings of an angel, he shall free us from oppression."

The pounding of noise almost deafened Thomas. He blinked away tears of an emotion he could not understand.

"Delivered on the wings of an angel, he shall free us from oppression."

It was time to return to earth.

homas found the knife in his inner shirt. He twisted against the shoulder straps and reached behind him.

Slash. He tore open a slit in the white cloth of the kite. Wind whistled through and he sagged downward.

Another slash. Slowly, the kite began to drop as its resistance to the wind lessened.

Foot by foot it dropped. As Thomas neared the ground, he began to loosen the straps around his shoulders. Then, just before the kite could die completely, he released himself and cut through the twine. The kite bobbed upward as Thomas fell. It drifted away in the darkness, too obscure to be seen for what it was.

He rolled with impact and stood immediately.

The crowd, with Sir William at the front and Tiny John at his side, advanced in a wave toward him.

"Delivered on the wings of an angel, he shall free us from oppression! Delivered on the wings of an angel, he shall free us from oppression!"

Thomas held up his right hand.

Instant silence at the front of the crowd. The silence rolled backward as each wave of villagers took its cue from the wave in front.

Within a minute, it was quiet enough for Thomas to hear his own thudding heart.

What do I say? None of my dreams prepared me for a moment like this!

Sir William rescued him.

"Thomas," he called, "Thomas of Magnus!"

In a great chant, the crowd took up those words. "Thomas of Magnus. Thomas of Magnus." Like thunder, his name rolled inside the castle walls.

Then Thomas remembered. Katherine!

He held up his hand again.

Again, the silence sifted backward from him.

"Sir William," Thomas cried, "the gate is open with half the soldiers outside. If you take it now, they will be unable to return."

Sir William understood immediately. *The army was divided already! The battle is half won!* It took little urging for him to gather a hundred men.

"Wait," Thomas cried again. "They have outside the girl Katherine. Bargain for her life."

The knight nodded briskly, and moved forward. One hundred angry men followed.

Thomas closed his eyes briefly. *What had he seen from his perch in the sky? Soldiers scurrying to their last retreat, the keep itself, four stories tall and unassailable.*

Tonight, these villagers were an army, unified by emotion and hope. Therefore, the remaining soldiers would not fight. They knew, as did Thomas, that tomorrow, or the day after, these fierce emotions would fade.

When that happened, these villagers would no longer be a solid army, prepared to die in a fight for freedom. Then once again a handful of trained fighters would be able to conquer and dominate hundreds of people.

The battle must be won tonight!

Thomas thought hard. Then it struck him. *If we cannot reach the soldiers tonight, they must not be able to reach us later.*

Thomas cast his eyes toward the keep. Unlike the castle walls, it had not been designed for soldiers to fight downward from above. The solution, once it hit him, was obvious.

"Good people of Magnus!"

Whatever shuffling of impatience there was in the crowd stopped immediately.

"Enough blood has been shed within these walls. Enough cruel oppression. Enough pain and bitterness. Tomorrow's dawn brings a new age in Magnus!"

The roar began, *"Delivered on the wings of an angel, he shall free us from oppression!"*

Thomas held up his hand again. "Our captors, now captive, shall be treated with kindness!"

To this, there was low grumbling.

"Do you not remember the pain inflicted on you?" Thomas shouted. "Then it is double the sin, knowing full well the pain, to inflict it in return."

Immediate silence, then murmurings of agreement. "We have a wise and kind ruler!" a voice yelled from the middle of the mob.

"Wise and kind! Wise and kind!"

Again, Thomas requested silence. "Furthermore," he shouted, "we shall not inflict injury upon ourselves by attempting to storm the keep."

A hum of questions reached him.

"Instead," Thomas shouted, "we shall wait until the remaining army surrenders." Before he could be interrupted again, Thomas picked a large man from the front of the crowd. "You, my good man, gather two hundred. Arm yourselves with spades and shovels and meet me in front of the keep in five minutes."

He pointed at another. "You, gather fifty men and all the tar and kindling in the village."

Sir William approached him with long strides. "Our men have barricaded the remaining soldiers outside the walls," he said with a grim furrow across his forehead.

"Yet there is no sign of the girl Katherine. Alive or dead."

Thomas beat his side once with his right fist. *This is no time to show pain or mourning,* he told himself. *Those around me must feel nothing but joy.*

He made his face appear expressionless under the bright lights of hundreds of torches.

"We cannot forsake the kingdom for one person," he told Sir William. "Not until this battle is complete shall I begin the search."

He gave his final command, "The rest must follow me and remain as guards. We do not want to tempt the soldiers to leave the keep and fight. Enough blood has been shed within the walls of Magnus!"

It took until noon the next day—
and three shifts of 100 men—to complete
Thomas's plan for bloodless warfare. When
it was finished, the keep had effectively
been isolated from the rest of the village
within the castle walls.

The men had dug a shallow moat around
the keep, throwing the dirt to the village
side to add to the barricade. Thomas then
had the moat filled with tar and pitch and
kindling. Standing guard, every twelve
paces, were men armed with torches. To
give them time to lead their normal lives,
their duty shifts were to run only four
hours each. There was no shortage of vol-
unteers. Day and night, each shift of men

twelve paces apart would guard the moat.

After the final barrel of pitch had oozed into the moat, Thomas called loudly upward at the keep. "Who wishes to speak to the new Lord of Magnus?"

All of the village stood gathered behind Thomas. Tomorrow, or the day after, they might resume normal village life if the siege dragged on. Today, however, was a day to behold. A new lord—one who had already shown wisdom and consideration for the life of men—was about to dictate terms of surrender to the old lord.

Thomas did not disappoint them.

A single face appeared from the third floor. "I am the captain."

Thomas said, "Not a single soldier shall die. But we will not provide food nor water. You may surrender when you wish. Be warned, however, should you decide to counterattack, the moat will impede any battle rush upon the village. And as you struggle to cross the pitch, it shall be set aflame!"

"We have heard you deal with fairness," the captain replied.

Thomas frowned in puzzlement.

"One of our men thanks you for his life," the captain explained.

Yes. The prison guard they had left with Waleran. And what has become of that spy...

"When you are prepared to surrender," Thomas instructed, "one of your men must deliver all your weapons to the edge of the moat. Then, and only then, will we build you a bridge to the safety of the village and to food and water."

Thomas paused. "Your lord will also be granted his life upon surrender."

The captain said, "That will not be necessary. Nor will a prolonged siege."

"What is that you say?"

"There is a tunnel on the far side of the walls which leads to the lake. The former lord of Magnus fled with two others during the night. We wish to surrender immediately."

❧

"Fare thee well, Thomas."

"I wish that it were not this way," Thomas replied to Sir William.

The knight smiled his ironic half smile. Beside him, his horse, a great roan stallion given from the stables of Magnus, danced and shook its mane with impatience.

"Thomas," Sir William said, "we are both men of the world. We do not 'wish.' We attempt to change what we know can be changed, we accept what cannot be changed, and we always strive for the wisdom to know the difference. In this case—" the smile broadened—"my departure cannot be changed."

Thomas held his head straight. If the knight would call him a man, he must fight the lump in his throat. "After a month in Magnus, you still dispense advice."

"Listen, puppy," the knight growled. "You may be lord of Magnus—and a good one, I might add—but you are never too old for good advice."

The new lord of Magnus squinted into the morning sun to blaze into his memory his last look at the knight. Not for the first time did he wonder about the scar on Sir William's face. Or where he went. Or from where he had arrived.

Thomas did not voice those questions.

Had the knight wanted any of that known, he surely would have revealed it by now.

So Thomas merely stood calmly, watched, and fought the sadness of departure.

An early breeze gently flapped the knight's colors against the stallion. Behind them, at the other end of the narrow land bridge, lay the walls of Magnus. Ahead, the winding trail that would lead Sir William up into the moors.

"I thank you for all your good advice," Thomas said in a quiet voice. "Without it, I would have foundered."

Thomas knew too well the truth of his words. Within hours of forcing the soldiers to surrender a month earlier, Thomas had discovered a position as lord meant much more than simply accepting tribute. No, the lord of a manor or village was also administrator, sometimes judge, sometimes jailer.

It was more difficult yet for a lord newly established. Sir William had first guided Thomas through the task of selecting his army from the soldiers. Those who swore loyalty remained. Those who didn't normally were skinned alive by flogging, or worse if the lord chose. Thomas had not. He did not want any men pretending loyalty merely to escape death. As a result, most of the men had been eager to serve a new master with such kindness and common sense.

Day by day, Sir William had taken Thomas through his new tasks as lord. Day by day, Thomas had grown more confident, and along with it, earned the confidence of the villagers. Had any of the villagers had doubts about their new lord because of his youth—even after his delivery on the wings of an angel and the way he had led them to victory—the doubts quickly disappeared. Thomas truly was Lord of Magnus.

As lord, he hid from public view his grief. Katherine had not been found. Nor had she appeared. Nor had there been any trace of the mute girl.

Even Tiny John, sent among the villagers who had befriended him, could not find a clue to the mute girl's disappearance.

His thoughts must have become obvious in those moments of farewell.

"You brood once more." Sir William's voice interrupted his thoughts. "Perhaps the time is not ready for my departure."

Thomas forced a grin. "You might remain? So that I must endure more of your nagging? I think not. Be on your way, and may, may..."

"May *God* be with me?" Sir William teased. "At least progress has been made. You are now ready to call upon Him to guard both you and me?"

Thomas smiled tightly. He *had* spent much time considering Katherine's strong faith. And he could not forget that during his worst moment in the air, he had cried out to the God he thought he did not believe.

Before the farewell moment could become awkward, Sir William mounted his horse.

"I thank you for my life," Sir William said with a salute.

The drumming of the horse's hooves remained with Thomas all of that day.

The next morning, at sunrise, two soldiers escorted the mute girl into the keep of the castle and she spoke her first words to Thomas.

y name is Isabelle," she said with a bow.

"Isabelle," Thomas repeated softly. He did not rise from his large chair in the front hall, despite his flood of joy. No lord did during an audience.

She stood in front of him in the front hall of the keep. Tapestries hung on the walls. The fireplace crackled, for even in the summer, mornings were cool. Two soldiers guarded the entrance, stiffly unmoving with eyes straight forward.

Tiny John bobbed into the room. All guards knew he had privilege at any time.

"I heard she was back," he blurted with wide eyes. He glanced her up and down and whistled.

"She's a marvel of beauty, she is!"

"She can also hear every word you say," Thomas observed with a dry smile. "This Isabelle is neither deaf nor mute."

"Aaack!" Tiny John spun on his heel and ran.

Tiny John had spoken truth of her beauty. The girl—*no, Isabelle*, Thomas told himself—did not wear rags. Instead, her long slim body was covered from neck to ankle in a clean white dress. Her long dark hair—before matted and tangled—now gleamed with health. The same beautifully etched high cheekbones. The same mysterious eyes. And the same haunting half smile.

She had become as much a woman in the previous month as Thomas had grown toward manhood with his new responsibilities as Lord of Magnus.

He wanted to weep with joy. Instead, he dismissed the soldiers. Too much, he was conscious of the dignity required as lord.

When they were alone, he whispered it again. "Isabelle."

"Yes, my lord."

"Please, 'Thomas.'"

She lowered her head, looked upward, and said shyly, "Yes, Thomas."

He wanted to throw himself into her arms. His heart pounded at the strange feelings he had tried to forget during the previous month.

"Isabelle," he started. Although he could will himself to remain in his chair, he could not keep the hushed wonder from his tone. "Your return is a miracle. Yet I am flooded with questions. Where have you been? How is it you prospered while away? And how is it you now speak and hear?"

She straightened her shoulders and looked him directly in the eyes. "There is much to tell. Will you listen, lord?"

He smiled. "Gladly."

Her smile—a promise and a reward in one—drew from him a silent marveling inward gasp. He managed to keep his face motionless.

"I, like you, am an orphan. My parents perished in a fire when I was a baby. I am told the villagers did not think it worth their while to preserve me. After all, I was only a girl. But a lonely old woman, one who was truly mute and deaf, defeated them. She fought for me. The villagers, who suspected she was a witch, dared not disagree and so she raised me. Then died when I was ten. With her gone, the villagers were free to chase me away."

Thomas nodded. His heart ached with growing love for her. *She was an outcast too. Together, they might...*

"Because the old lady could not hear, I learned early to speak with my hands. And when I was forced to travel from village to village, seeking food and shelter, I soon discovered the advantages of posing as mute and deaf. It earned pity. Also, I learned not to trust, and being mute and deaf put me behind walls that no person could break."

Isabelle faltered and looked down at her hands. "Not even you, Thomas, wanted me. You saved us all from death by hanging, and you only wanted the knight."

"That is no longer true," he said quickly and with some guilt

"So I chose to remain mute and deaf. Yet often, I would see you glancing at me, and my heart would wonder..."

Thomas finally moved from his chair. He approached her, and took her hands in his.

"Perhaps," he said gently, "your heart was hearing mine."

Moments of silence that seemed to roar in his ears.

"When you were arrested," she began again, "I fled Magnus. After three days of travel, I reached the dales near the town of York. I had not eaten. I had barely slept. I hailed the first passing carriage and begged for a chance to work. The lady inside took pity. She fed and clothed me, and arranged for me to work as a maid in her kitchen. When word reached me of the fall of Magnus—"

"Word has reached the outer world?" Thomas interrupted sharply.

She bowed her head again. "Yes."

This can only mean the Earl of York will arrive soon, Thomas realized with a pang of urgency. *Am I prepared to keep this small kingdom against the forces of the larger one around it?*

He kept his face still. "So you braved the moors and returned."

"Yes," Isabelle said. "My heart could not rest until it discovered the answer."

"Answer?"

She tightened her grip on his hands. "Yes. Answer. Did I belong to you. Or had I been fooling myself about your glances."

"I am the only fool," Thomas said gallantly. "Not to have searched the world for you."

She did not hesitate. She threw her arms around his neck.

Thomas felt on his neck her warm skin and—pressed tight as she was—the cool circle of her medallion.

Take them with you. The old man's words at the hanging. *It will guarantee you a safe journey to Magnus.*

Even as Thomas held her, his mind raced with thoughts and questions.

Slowly, ever so slowly, he released her.

A single tear dropped from his eye.

"Isabelle," he croaked, "I wish it were not so."

What had Sir William said upon departure? *We do not wish. We attempt to change what we know can be changed. We accept what cannot be changed, and we always strive for the wisdom to know the difference between the two.*

"You must answer me these further questions," Thomas continued in the same pained voice. "Why have you lied to me about your childhood? Who are you? And who placed you among us? Was it the old man at the gallows?"

"I, I do not understand."

Do not wish. Attempt to change what you know can be changed.

He forced the words from his mouth. "If you do not answer, you shall spend your remaining days condemned to the same dungeon you arranged for me and the knight."

Sigmund Brouwer

It took five days for Isabelle to realize Thomas was not bluffing. Five days of darkness. Five days of solitude. Five days with the endless rustling of rats in straw.

When she next appeared in front of him in the hall, her hair was matted, and her eyes only held wildness of fear, not mystery.

Thomas too had dark circles under his eyes. Sleep did not come easily in the anguish of doubt.

Yet there was the medallion and the time in the dungeon...

Thomas again dismissed the guards at the entrance, and rose himself to shut the doors behind them.

He waited for her to speak

The silence stretched. Still, he waited behind her and said nothing.

Finally, she spoke without turning. Her voice broke upon the words. "How is it you know?"

At that, Thomas sighed. A tiny hope had flickered that he was wrong, that he could still trust her.

"Your medallion," he said. "What a blunder to leave it around your neck upon your return."

She clutched it automatically.

"Do not fear," Thomas said heavily. "I have seen it already, the day that Tiny John lifted it from you on the moors. The strange symbol upon it matches the symbol engraved in the scepter I found below the former lord's bed, now mine. I forgot seeing it, until your return reminded me."

Isabelle shivered and hugged herself.

"Moreover," Thomas continued, "there was the soldiers' attack outside the walls of Magnus the night I was delivered on 'the wings of an angel.' How did they know to venture outside the walls? I had not been followed. No sentry could have seen me or Katherine. You or the knight or Tiny John were the only ones to know that I had with me on my way here a bag filled with the means to conquer Magnus. You or the knight or Tiny John were the only ones to know I had left it outside the castle walls."

Isabelle turned to face him.

"And our arrest," Thomas said. "It could not have been a coincidence. Or the fact that a spy had already been planted in the dungeon ahead of us. The knowledge of our presence in Magnus could only have come from you, the person who disappeared our first morning here to return with a bowl of porridge to explain your absence."

Isabelle nodded.

The implications staggered Thomas. *Isabelle's nearness to Thomas had already been planned before the hanging and the rescue of Sir William! Again, it circled back to the old man and his knowledge at the gallows!*

"Why? How?" Thomas said, almost quiet with despair. "My plans to conquer Magnus were a dream, kept only to myself. How did the lord know—"

"Why?" she said calmly. "Duty. I am Lord Richard's daughter."

"Daughter! You were one of the three fig-

ures to escape the night of the conquering!"
Thomas stopped, puzzled. "No one recognized you here when you arrived with us."

"Do you think over the years that the lord
of Magnus would dare let his daughter wan-
der the streets among a people who hated
him? Of course I was not recognized."

Thomas shook his head. "And duty dic-
tated you return and pretend love for me?"

She nodded.

"How were you to kill me?" Thomas
asked with bitterness. "Poison as I drank to
your health? A lady-like dagger thrust in
my ribs during a long embrace?"

A half sob escaped Isabelle. "Those...
those were my father's commands. I am
still unsure whether I could have fulfilled
them."

Thomas shrugged, although at her
admission the last pieces of his heart fell
into a cold black void. "No matter, of
course. I cared little for you."

She blinked, stung.

"Go on," Thomas said with the same
lack of tone. "From the beginning. At the
gallows."

"As you have guessed," she then said, "it

was arranged I would be on the gallows. My father feared a threat to his kingdom. And he did not believe the knight would die."

That was the greatest mystery. From the beginning, the lord of the very kingdom Thomas intended to take had forseen his every move.

"How did your father know? Did he instruct the old man to appear at the gallows? Or is it reversed—did the old man instruct your father of my intentions?"

"Old man?" Isabelle stared at Thomas for long moments. Then she threw her head back in laughter. When she finished, and found her breath again, she said, almost with disbelief, "You truly do not know."

Thomas gritted his teeth. "I truly do not know *what*."

"I was not there because of you. You were not the threat my father feared. I was there because of the knight."

Because of the knight with the unknown background!

Isabelle kept her voice flat. "My father sometimes used cruel methods to maintain his power. I did not approve nor disapprove. This is a difficult world. I am told that when my father first overthrew the lord of Magnus..."

Thomas gritted his teeth again. *Sarah's parents.*

"...that he publicly branded each opposing soldier and knight. Then he had them flogged to death. One escaped. The most loyal and most valiant fighter of them all."

She let those words hang while Thomas grasped the truth.

"Sir William!"

"Yes. Sir William. When my father received word Sir William had returned to this land, he paid a great sum of money to have the sacred chalices stolen and placed among his belongings."

"You were sent to the hanging to be a spy should he be rescued. How did your father know the rescue would occur?"

"He guessed it might. And my father wanted to take no chances. The hangman had instructions to release me if no rescue occurred and the knight died on the gallows."

Thomas paced to the far side of the room. *"Why? Why did he foresee a rescue?" Nothing could be more important to Thomas than this. If*

Isabelle could explain why, it would lead to the old man and how anyone knew Thomas would be at the hanging.

"Thomas," she began, "there is a great circle of conspiracy. Much larger than you and I. My father too acted upon the commands of another. And there is much at stake."

"You are speaking in circles."

"Because I know only what I have guessed after a lifetime in Magnus. Haven't you wondered why this castle is set so securely so far away from the outer world. Why would anyone bother attacking a village here? Yet an impenetrable castle was founded. And by no less a wizard than—"

The door exploded open.

Time fragmented before Thomas's eyes. *Geoffrey the candlemaker! At a full run with short club extended! Startled guards in half motion behind him! Club thrown downward! Thomas beginning to dive at flashing dagger! Too late!*

Much too late. And Thomas, half stunned by his full-length dive, raised his head in time to see the first guard with an uplifted sword.

"No! Don't—" Thomas began to roar—
"He must not be harmed."

Too late again. Geoffrey fell into a limp
huddle. Beside him in a smaller huddle,
Isabelle.

Geoffrey's arm and hand scraped the
floor in a feeble twitch.

Thomas could only stare at the fingers
and ring now inches from his face.

He finally rose in the horrified silence
shared by both guards.

"My lord, we did not know—"

Thomas waved a weary hand to stop the
soldier's voice.

The unsteady rise and fall of both chests
showed neither Geoffrey nor Isabelle had
been killed. Thomas bent and gently took
the medallion from Isabelle's neck. Then
he compared it to the ring on Geoffrey's
hand.

The match was identical.

Chapter Twenty-Eight ~ Part Three

ach dawn found Thomas on the eastern ramparts of the castle walls. The guards knew by now to respect his need for privacy; each morning the sentry for that part of the wall would respectfully retreat at the sight of the new lord of Magnus approaching.

This hour gave Thomas what little peace he could find. The wind had yet to rise on the moors. The cry of birds carried from far across the lake surrounding Magnus. First rays of sun edged over the top of the eastern slope and began to reflect off the calm water. Behind Thomas, the town lay silent.

It was the time of day that he searched his own emptiness.

"Sarah," he spoke to his long-dead friend. "The castle has been taken from the brutal conqueror who killed your parents. That was my promise to you as you lay dying. Now fulfilled. Yet why do I feel so restless."

The morning did not answer.

He could keep a brave and resolute face as new Lord of Magnus. He always did during the busy days with the villagers. Yet in the quiet times, there were too many questions.

There is so little that I know, Thomas thought.

An old man cast the sun into darkness and directed me here from the gallows. The old man knew Isabelle was a spy, the old man knew my dream of conquering Magnus. Who was that old man. Will he ever reappear?

A valiant and scarred knight befriended me and helped me win the castle that once belonged to his own lord. Then departed. Why?

A crooked candlemaker and the daughter of the lord we vanquished remain in the dungeons of Magnus, refusing to speak, though long since recovered from the blows which rendered them unconscious. What conspiracy was Isabelle about to reveal? Why is she silent now? And why do they share the same strange symbol?

And what fate has fallen upon Katherine?

There is so much I must do, Thomas thought.

There are the books filled with priceless knowledge, able to give a young man the power to conquer kingdoms. They must be brought safely to the castle.

The Earl of York has heard that Magnus has fallen to me. He will arrive to exact tribute or begin a seige. All of Magnus must be prepared.

And I must not cease in searching—without the villagers aware—for the secrets of Magnus.

Thomas closed his eyes.

For a moment, Katherine's voice echoed in his mind. He kept his eyes closed, desperate for any comfort.

What had she once said? *You and I are threads, Thomas. We cannot see God's plan for us.*

Thomas opened his eyes. The sun had broken over the top of the faraway hill, spilling rays across the dips and swells of the land.

Thomas smiled. *Oh, that there were a God with enough love and wisdom to watch over all our follies.*

He speculated with wonder on that thought for many long minutes. He thought of Katherine's braveness and conviction. He thought of his own confusion.

Suddenly, Thomas spun on his heels and marched from the ramparts.

He strode through the village streets and came to a small stone building near the center market square.

There, he banged against the rough wooden door.

A strong voice answered and the door opened to show an elderly man with gray hair combed straight back

"My lord," he said without fear. "Come inside, please. We are graced with your presence."

They moved to the nave at the front of the church. Sunlight streamed through the eastern windows and cut sharp shadows across both their faces. In the man's eyes, Thomas saw nothing of the greed he had witnessed for those many years at the abbey. It was enough for Thomas to finally speak.

"Father," Thomas said. "Help me in my unbelief."

AUTHOR'S NOTE

For two thousand years—far north and east of London—the ancient English towns of Pickering, Thirsk, and Helmsley, and their castles, have guarded a line on the lowland plains between the larger centers of Scarborough and York.

In the beginning, Scarborough, with its high North Sea cliffs, was a Roman signal post. From there, sentries could easily see approaching barbarian ships, and were able to relay messages from Pickering to Helmsley to Thirsk, the entire fifty miles inland to the boundary outpost of York, where other troops waited—always ready—for any inland invasions.

When their empire fell, the Romans in England succumbed to the Anglo-Saxons, great savage brutes in tribal units who conquered as warriors, and over the generations became farmers. The Anglo-Saxons in turn suffered defeat by raiding Vikings, who in turn lost to the Norman knights from France with their thundering war horses.

Through those hundreds and hundreds of years, that line from Scarborough to York never diminished in importance.

Some of England's greatest and richest abbeys—religious retreats for monks—accumulated their wealth on the lowland plains along that line. Rievaulx Abbey, just outside Helmsley, contained 250 monks and owned vast estates of land which held over 13,000 sheep.

But directly north lay the moors—high, desolate and windswept hills.

No towns or abbeys tamed the moors, which reached east hundreds of square miles to the craggy cliffs of the cold grey North Sea.

Each treeless and windswept moor plunged into deep dividing valleys of lush greenness that only made the heather-covered heights appear more harsh. The ancients called these North York moors "Blackamoor."

Thus, in the medieval age of chivalry, 250 years after the Norman knights had toppled the English throne, this remoteness and isolation protected Blackamoor's earldom of Magnus from the prying eyes of King Edward II and the rest of his royal court in London.

Magnus, as a kingdom within a kingdom, was small in comparison to the properties of England's greater earls. This smallness too was protection. Hard to reach and easy to defend, British and Scottish kings chose to overlook it, and in practical terms, it had as much independence as a separate country.

Magnus still had size, however. Its castle commanded and protected a large village and many vast moors. Each valley between the moors averaged in length a full day's travel by foot. Atop the moors, great flocks of sheep grazed on the tender green shoots of heather. The valley interiors supported cattle and cultivated plots of land, farmed by peasants nearly made slaves by the yearly tribute exacted from their crops. In short, with sheep and wool and cattle and land, Magnus was not a poor earldom, and well worth ruling.

Magnus itself cannot be found in any history book. Nor can Thomas be found. Nor his nurse Sarah, the wandering knight Sir William, Katherine, Geoffrey the Candlemaker, Tiny John, nor others of the collection of friends and foes of Thomas. Yet many of the more famous people and events found throughout its story shaped the times of that world, as historians may easily confirm.

HISTORICAL NOTES

Readers may find it of interest that in the times in which the "Winds of Light" series is set, children were considered adults much earlier than now. By church law, for example, a bride had to be at least 12, a bridegroom 14. (This suggests that on occasion marriage occurred at an even earlier age!)

It is not so unusual, then, to think of Thomas of Magnus becoming accepted as a leader by the age of 14; many would already consider him a man simply because of his age. Moreover, other "men" also became leaders at remarkably young ages during those times. King Richard II, for example, was only 14 years old when he rode out to face the leaders of the Peasants' Revolt in 1381.

More specifically, following are more historical notes on *Wings of an Angel*:

Chapter Two

Although there is no specific mention of an eclipse at this time in historical records, it does not necessarily mean that the eclipse did not occur. Scientific observations were almost non-existent, and a partial eclipse could well have briefly darkened that part of England without an official recording.

Chapter Nine

Gunpower had been used by the Chinese since the tenth century A.D. Despite that, it was not until the year 1313 that any European "discovered" its explosive power; credit for its invention there is commonly given to a German friar named Berthold Schwarz. Is it possible, however, that knowledge of its ingredients may have been known to other Europeans shortly before that time?

Chapter Ten

Wades Causeway is a preserved stretch of Roman road which may still be traveled today in the Wheeldale Moor of the Yorkshire area of England. It was built almost two thousand years ago by the first Roman soldiers to reach Yorkshire in the year A.D. 70, and probably reached all the way to the coast. One of the reasons for the great success of the Roman soldiers as they conquered all of England was their roads, which let them move their armies with great efficiency.

Chapter Eleven

The number of fighting knights in England by the year A.D. 1300 has been estimated to be less than 2,000. There were other land-owners who were called "knights" because they owed military service to the barons and kings above them, but they were country gentlemen, not members of a military elite.

Chapter Twelve

The barbican was an outwork of stone built to protect the gatehouse or entrance into the castle area. Sometimes it was a wall of stone leading up to the gatehouse, and later, as barbicans became more elaborate with their own turrets and drawbridges, they actually became outer gatehouses.

Chapter Thirteen

Although some scholars disagree, it is commonly held that Sun Tzu—a Chinese general and military genius who lived hundreds of years before Christ was born—compiled a book of his military theories and philosophies. This book has survived relatively unchanged for over 2,000 years. It is probable that this is the "greatest general of a faraway land" to which Thomas refers in his thoughts. Today, readers may find all of Sun Tzu's surviving military advice in a book titled *The Art of War*.

Chapter Twenty-Two

Marco Polo is an Italian explorer who reached Cathay (now known as China) in A.D. 1275. He served the Mongolian ruler Kublai Khan for many years and returned to Venice 111 A.D. 1295. During his travels, Marco Polo noted a Chinese custom, which consisted of sending a huge man-carrying kite into the air before a ship set sail on a long voyage.

❦